The Siege of Gibraltar

May - June 1941

A Misfit Squadron Novel

Simon Brading

First published 2020

This edition published 2024

ISBN: 978-1-917470-06-3

For James,
who delayed the completion of this book for many months,
but made them some of the best of my life.

PROLOGUE

'Dammit, Lang, where's that aspirin?'

'Here, sir.'

The butler lifted the silver tray fractionally to call his master's attention to the small bottle of white pills and the crystal glass full of water sitting on it.

Gruber grabbed the pills and shook two of them into his hand. After a moment's hesitation he shook four more out - he wasn't going to let such a small thing as a hangover ruin his big day. He popped them into his mouth in one go and gulped the water to wash them down.

'Ah!' He smacked his lips then slammed the glass back down on the tray. The butler winced as his arms were jerked and Gruber looked at him. 'What's the matter with you?'

'Nothing, sir.'

The pain in the man's eyes and the bandage wrapped around his head made a lie out of his words, but Gruber was too busy to notice. He turned back to the mirror and continued to button up his dress uniform tunic, smiling at the imposing figure gazing back at him.

He'd always liked the "bad guy" aesthetic far more than that of the insipid "good guys" he'd played and the Hollywoodland costume designer had followed his instructions well, incorporating all the little touches he'd demanded, like the silver death's head buttons he'd worn as the pirate captain in *The Sky is Not the Limit* and the crimson lanyard, which had been a stroke of genius, even if he did say so himself. The designer had even managing to put platforms into his impressive but impractical riding boots, which gave him an extra few centimetres, allowing him to look down on most men and stand out in a crowd - extremely important when hunting for a night's "entertainment".

He did up the last button and waited impatiently while Lang brushed him down and made sure everything was just right. 'Come on, come on.'

'Finished, sir.'

'At last.' Gruber stalked from the room and out onto the Sicilian airbase.

Hölle was immediately outside the small building that served as his private ready room - he had ordered it to be put on the concrete path around the airfield that was usually reserved for pedestrian traffic and small vehicles, so that he wouldn't have to walk across the dew-wet grass. He paused to scrutinise the machine and grunted in satisfaction; what little damage he'd taken during the previous day's fighting had been repaired and the paintwork had been buffed up to a high shine. The team of mechanics he'd had working all night had done a passable job of making sure that his aircraft would be at its best for the cameras recording the day's historical events for posterity and the people of Prussia.

Those men were lined up outside, ready for his inspection. They had come to attention and saluted when he'd appeared, but he ignored them completely and went directly to Hölle. He used a small step ladder to climb up onto the wing, then stepped through the door in the side of the cockpit and sat gingerly, careful not to wrinkle his trousers. A mechanic held out his helmet and he grabbed it, but stuffed it into the storage compartment behind him; he didn't want to spoil his hair and besides, he wouldn't need it for such a short trip in skies that belonged to him. He didn't worry about strapping in, either, he just immediately opened the throttle, sending the far too slow-moving mechanic tumbling from the wing. Hölle leapt forwards eagerly and Gruber swung onto the grass, then pushed the lever fully forwards. He powered past the line of Blutsaugers and accelerated to takeoff speed, not bothering to go to the downwind end of the airfield; the base had been constructed for bombers and there was more than enough room to play with.

After a few short seconds Hölle leapt gleefully into the air, mirroring Gruber's own feelings, although he did suffer a moment of queasiness as his stomach dropped, the aspirin not yet having taken full effect. He ignored it, though; nothing was going to spoil such an auspicious day - for the first time in his short but illustrious military career he would be personally accepting the surrender of enemy forces. Until then, he'd always had to play second fiddle to someone else, but the Kaiser had finally given him his due and placed him in overall command of the efforts to take Malta. He had put that authority to spectacularly good use and done what the Italians hadn't been able to.

There had been a cost, of course, paid mostly by the *Reichsflotte*, the navy, but he himself had suffered too, and he glanced over his wing at the wreckage sprawled on the southern shore of the island, only a few kilometres from the air base he'd appropriated.

Bertha, the airship that had served as the base for his squadron since the start of the war, had crash-landed on Sicily for the second time in just a few months. It had been in a much less controlled fashion this time, though, after sustaining major damage from the guns of Malta and it looked like her stay on the ground would be rather more permanent than the previous one. Gruber hadn't read the full damage report from the admiral - he hadn't had time, what with the celebrations that had taken place the night before - but he gathered that the huge airship would be grounded for quite some time and that many of the parts would have to be fabricated especially in the factory where she had been built. He didn't care one bit, though; Malta was now his and so were the Misfits trapped on the island - after the few of them that survived had surrendered to him he would fly back to Berlin with them and parade them around. And he didn't need Bertha for that.

The trip to Malta at maximum unwind took almost no time at all, but as soon as Gruber was within sight of land he slowed, allowing the rest of his squadron to catch up with him. He hadn't taken his aircraft very high, only a thousand feet - without a flightsuit or even a thick coat it would have been too cold - but now, as he approached the Maltese capital of Valletta, he brought the formation of sixteen bright red aircraft even lower, wanting the people to get a good look at their conqueror. He flew down the length of the harbour, past the wreckage of the Royal Navy ships, then banked around to make a large circle over the rest of the city, taking in the fortifications, both modern and medieval, studded with multiple anti-aircraft gun emplacements and the huge anti-ship artillery pieces, none of which had done anything to stop him.

He was quite tempted to loiter over the ravaged and broken city for a while longer and perhaps do some aerobatics, but there was important business to be done, so once the circuit was finished he levelled off and accelerated back to top speed, heading south towards his final destination - the Royal Aviator Corps base at Hal Far, where the Misfits were stationed and where he had arranged to accept their surrender.

It was only five miles from Valletta to Hal Far and about a minute later they arrived over the bare airfield. Gruber brought his aircraft straight in to land and taxied towards where several hundred people were waiting for him - the massed ranks of the troops who had ensured the airfield was safe, a group of *Reichsflotte* officers, led by the admiral, and, of course, the defeated.

He brought Hölle to a halt in front of the crowd and swung around, uncaring that the backwash from his airscrew was buffeting them. He shut down as quickly as he could, then climbed out and jumped off the back of his wing as athletically as he could, making sure to present a heroic picture to the movie cameras he could hear whirring away to each side. He straightened his back, made sure his uniform hadn't rucked up on the journey, then strode towards the admiral. Half-way there his step faltered and the grin slipped from his face when he realised that something was wrong.

There were no British officers with the admiral - the men with him were dressed in suits or the black robes of priests.

He stopped in his tracks. Now that he came to think about it, none of the wrecks in the harbour had seemed quite big enough to be the aircraft carrier that had brought the Misfits.

Something broke inside him and a red mist descended in front of his eyes as he stalked forward. Heedless of the movie cameras set up only metres away he grabbed the front of the admiral's coat and screamed at him. *'Where the hell are my Misfits?'*

CHAPTER 1

14th May 1941

Gwen came awake very slowly. The nightmare she'd been caught in had been full of tearing metal and shattering glass and the klaxon blended in so well with it that it wasn't until Scarlet roughly shook her that she realised that it wasn't a part of it.

'Come on!'

'What is it? What's going on?'

'No idea,' a new voice came, that of Abby. 'But I want to be ready for anything. Gwen, Drake, Scarlet, get your flightsuits on, everyone else dress up warm. We're going up to the flight deck. I want everything ready to fly.'

With so many refugees from Malta crowding the Arturo, the Misfits had been forced to share their usual quarters and had packed into a single small room with bunk beds so there was no need for Abby to repeat her order elsewhere or shout it down a corridor.

Gwen rolled out of bed and stood up, just in time to be knocked off her feet as the Arturo shook.

The Misfits paused in dressing and looked at each other.

'Well, that can't be good.' Scarlet chuckled wryly, expressing what they were all thinking.

'This is a big ship,' said Drake. 'I'm sure it will take more than one explosion to...'

Three more impacts resounded through the Arturo in quick succession, sending them all staggering. Derek had had one leg lifted in the act of putting on his trousers and he fell, knocking over the half-dressed Abby and landing on top of her.

He blanched. 'I do beg your pardon.'

'That's quite alright, Derek, but would you please just bloody get off me already!'

The Misfits hurriedly finished dressing and rushed out. The doors to the other rooms were open and sailors were already coming out of them, milling around in confusion, but Abby bellowed at them.

'Coming through! Let us pass!'

Her authoritative voice, combined with the fact that everyone sharing the quarters with them knew exactly who they were, opened a path for them immediately and the pilots raced down the corridor and through the equally packed sitting area, heading for the exit.

The bulkhead door opened before they got to it, though, and a young Royal Navy officer appeared. He took one look at them and backed away, clearing the doorway, but fell in behind Abby as she raced past and up the stairs to the hangar deck.

'Captain's complements, ma'am, and would you ready your aircraft for takeoff, please?'

'That's what we're doing, Lieutenant. What's happening?'

'We've been hit by torpedoes, ma'am. That's all I know.'

'Is the ship in any danger?'

'I couldn't say, ma'am.'

'Find out, please.'

'I'll do my best, ma'am.' The officer pulled the bulkhead door leading to the hangar open. He waved the pilots through, then closed it after them and ran forwards towards the bridge.

Another explosion rocked them and when the noise had died down Abby turned to her squadron. 'If we're being hit by torpedoes during the night it's not likely to be aircraft, so we're probably not going to be needed to fight, but we might have to get out of here in a hurry. We're close to Gibraltar, so we can go there if we have to. Derek, Bruce, you'll be in Scarlet's pods. Tanya, you'll have to sit on Drake's lap, I'm afraid, but I'm sure that won't be too much of a hardship for you.'

'I think we can put up with that.' Drake grinned at Tanya.

'I think you should sit on my lap.' Tanya replied.

'Discuss it later.' Abby said. 'Here comes our man.'

She called their attention to the Lieutenant, who was sprinting towards them, dodging through the mechanics working on the Misfit aircraft.

He staggered to a halt in front of them, completely out of breath. 'Abandon ship,' he managed to gasp out. 'Evacuate to Gibraltar. Fifty-five miles, bearing two seven five.'

Even as the man spoke, the klaxon took on a more urgent, more strident tone.

There was a moment of stillness, but then all hell broke loose. The men and women performing routine tasks around the hangar all but disappeared, racing for the doors in the sides of the hangars, while the movements of the mechanics and fitters working to get the aircraft ready to fly became almost frantic.

'Get to your aircraft!' Abby shouted as she ran towards Dragon at the very front of the hangar. Most of the squadron followed her, but Gwen hesitated and shared a glance with Drake. 'Good luck, Digger.'

He nodded and gave her a wry smile. 'You too, Goosy. See you on the Rock.'

They both broke into a run, Gwen more awkwardly than Drake; the liquid pockets in the legs of the suit making the exercise much harder.

As she ran, Gwen found herself staggering slightly, unable to go in a straight line and feeling disorientated. At first she put it down to the remnants of her concussion, or having just woken up, but when a small tool cart wandered across her path, forcing her to dodge to avoid it, she realised that it wasn't her, it was the deck. It was becoming tilted.

'This is the captain speaking. The Arturo has been struck by enemy torpedoes and efforts to save her have failed. Abandon ship. Repeat, abandon ship. Good luck and see you all shoreside.'

Gwen barely heard Captain Hewer's words over the tannoy system; she was too busy trying to get to Excalibur without tripping over the tools and cables that suddenly seemed to be everywhere. She eventually made it and found Giuseppe, the young Maltese man who had taken over as her chief fitter, perched on the wing, waiting for her. She climbed up and into the cockpit and he leaned in to start strapping her in while she plugged herself into the heater and radio system.

'Everything good, Giuseppe?'

'Yes, ma'am. We finished the wiring this evening, so you're good to go.'

The Misfit Squadron fitters had been taking advantage of the aircraft being grounded to carry out long overdue repairs, fixing problems that had been lingering for weeks in some cases. Only that afternoon, several of the Duralumin panels had still been off Excalibur's tail while frayed control wires leading to the rudder and elevators were being replaced.

'Thank you.' Gwen finished her pre-fight checks and lifted her eyes to watch as Dragon was pushed forwards onto the lift, to take the short trip up to the front of the flight deck, but motion in the mirror over her head caught her eye and she craned her neck around in time to see Hummingbird take flight through the hole in the side of the ship.

She waited until it had disappeared into the darkness before turning back to Giuseppe. 'Do you know what you have to do to abandon ship?'

The young man grinned. 'Oh, yes. The Navy have been *very* thorough in making sure that everybody knows exactly what they have to do if something happens. We've had about a dozen drills since we boarded.'

Gwen winced, remembering the journey from Scotland to Muscovy. The Misfits had been put through half a dozen lifeboat drills in just the first week - being woken up by the quarterdeck bellows of Royal Navy officers in the middle of the night wasn't exactly her idea of fun.

'Good. Make sure you get your team to the lifeboats as soon as I'm gone.'

'Will do, ma'am. Good luck.'

The young man patted the side of the cockpit fondly, then jumped down from the wing. Seconds later the lift thumped back into place and he joined his team in pushing Excalibur onto it.

Gwen waved her thanks to the fitters, but then turned back and concentrated on the job at hand.

If taking off from the Arturo during the day was nerve-wracking due to the small deck and the sheer drop off the sides, doing it at night was absolutely terrifying, with only small red lamps every ten yards to show her where the edge of the deck was and just black beyond them. She couldn't hesitate or delay, though, not with Drake still needing to take off and, according to her artificial horizon, the Arturo's list becoming more pronounced every minute.

She bit her lip as something occurred to her.

Usually you started your takeoff run from the rear of an aircraft carrier because then its speed through the water was added to the aircraft's, allowing it to take off in a much shorter distance. The Arturo's engines were silent, though, and it wasn't moving, so Excalibur wouldn't be getting any help and if Gwen didn't do things right she might well struggle to reach sufficient airspeed to fly before she ran out of deck. That would obviously be bad, however there was one good thing about it, and that was that she didn't need to waste time taxiing to the stern for takeoff.

As soon as the lift reached the flight deck she swung around to line up with the centre of the two red lines and moved forwards just enough to get off the lift. She waved blindly at the darkness to her right, where one of the flight deck controllers should be and was relieved to receive a couple of blinks from a green light, the signal that there were no obstructions on the deck and she was clear to takeoff when she was ready.

Gwen made sure that her brakes were fully engaged, then pushed the throttle through the stops. The enormous airscrew began to thrum angrily, but she waited until Excalibur was growling and struggling against the restraint before giving her the freedom she wanted. The aircraft surged forward and raced through the darkness, pressing her back into her seat. She had a brief moment of panic when she realised that the tilted deck was making Excalibur drift to the side, but some quick footwork on the rudder brought her back on course before it was too late.

The lights marking the end of the deck flashed by almost before she saw them and the deck disappeared from underneath her. As she'd feared, Excalibur hadn't been able to reach takeoff speed and she dropped sickeningly, but Gwen was ready for it and she allowed the nose to fall slightly, sacrificing some of her precious height for speed. That was all the extra help that was needed and the wings bit almost immediately, turning Excalibur from a projectile into a living creature. Gwen pulled up slowly, carefully, gradually bringing the aircraft's nose to the horizon, then finally above it and into a shallow climb, before letting go of the breath she'd been holding and reporting in.

'Tinman. Badger Two is away.'

'Acknowledged, Badger Two.'

She turned onto the course the Lieutenant had given them and only then did she look back at the Arturo.

She stared, transfixed by the hellish sight.

The moon was only a couple of days past full and shining brightly, but she didn't need it to see the huge ship, lit as it was by the fires that raged in the lower decks, almost her entire length. Smoke boiled and swirled, painted red from within, and, as she watched, an explosion sent flames shooting out into the night, illuminating dozens of small white dots swarming away from it. With each passing second more and more of the boats were dropping into the water on all sides, but they seemed far too few to carry the thousands of people that had been forced to pack into the ship by the circumstances of their evacuation from Malta. The two destroyers, which had been trying to screen the carrier from just such an event, were racing down to her and would be able to aid the survivors, but Gwen knew that dozens, if not hundreds of people would be trapped by the flames, or would be too deep within the bowels of the ship to make it to the boats. They would meet their ends that night, to be forever entombed in the depths within their vessel.

Excalibur was taking her too far away now to make out any detail, but she kept her eyes on the carrier, trying to see the flight deck through the smoke wreathing around it, watching for Lion, Drake's aircraft. She thought she saw a dark dot come bursting through it, but she couldn't be sure it was him until the radio crackled in her ears.

'Tinman, this is Badger Three. I'm clear.'

'Acknowledged, Badger Three. All Badgers, this is Tinman, signing off.'

'Thank you, Tinman, good luck.' Abby waited a few seconds for a reply, but the controller in the Arturo was undoubtedly already on his way to the lifeboats, having only remained at his post long enough to see the Misfits clear, and all that came back was static, so she switched to the squadron channel. 'Right, then, Badgers, let's get ourselves to Gibraltar. I'll call in as soon as we get within range and as soon as we get clearance Badger Four can go straight in, but the rest of us will have to circle until first light. Are you comfortable to wait that long, Badger Three?'

'Roger, Leader, although I thought I'd just give Tanya my glidewings and chuck her out over the Rock.'

'From anyone else I'd be sure that was a joke, but I never know with you two.'

CHAPTER 2

Due to the nature of Hummingbird, Scarlet was able to land as soon as she got to Gibraltar, but the other Misfit aircraft had to circle over the Rock for a couple of hours, waiting for daylight before they tackled the unfamiliar and extremely unusual landing conditions.

As the sun reached the horizon the night receded and the peninsula they had last seen five months before was slowly revealed - the deceptively sleepy looking town, the port filled with the dozens of ships of the Gibraltar fleet, and the "Rock" itself, with its radar and radio masts and its multitude of artillery and anti-aircraft emplacements. Of the airbase there was no sign, though, but they hadn't expected there to be; RAC Gibraltar was hidden *within* the mountain itself.

Construction had begun on the base over twenty years earlier, just after the First Great War, and had taken over five years to complete.

First, a tunnel with a rectangular cross-section, eighty yards wide and fifty high, had been cut all the way through the Rock to form the runway. Three hundred yards up the mountain and almost directly below the summit, it ran twenty degrees or so clockwise of east to west, which put it more or less in line with the two main prevailing winds, the "Levante" and the "Poniente", and meant that aircraft could almost always take off into the wind. It was easily wide enough for the largest of aircraft, including Dreadnought, and long enough at half a mile for even the heaviest to have room to stop.

Once the runway was completed, the British engineers had again cut into the rock, tunnelling northwards to build a row of four hangars right next to it. One hundred and fifty yards wide and one hundred yards deep, with ten-yard-high ceilings, each was big enough for eight fighter squadrons or up to three bomber squadrons. Smaller rooms, only forty yards square, were also excavated on either end of the row for the workshops where major repairs could be carried out, or new aircraft constructed if needed from the abundance of materials in the store rooms leading off of them.

Beyond these cavernous spaces, much smaller rooms with lower ceilings were then carved out for everything else an RAC base needed, like offices, design rooms, weapons workshops, a radio room and a large mess.

Finally, a whole other complex was constructed, in what space was left over, to serve as the living quarters for the men and women stationed there, but also as a refuge for the entire population of Gibraltar if it were ever necessary.

The Misfits had never laid eyes on any of that - so that the winds that blew almost constantly weren't always whistling through the base, the runway was closed off when not in use by immense iron doors at each end, their outer surfaces camouflaged to appear part of the mountain. Those doors had been shut when the Arturo had sailed by in January, so the pilots didn't know exactly where the base was and, no matter how much they peered at the slopes and sheer faces on either side of the Rock, they couldn't find it, at least until a long dark horizontal line appeared suddenly, shockingly, in the sheer eastern face of the mountain.

The slit widened quickly, the earth and rock of the mountain seemingly sliding upwards, until it was a gaping black hole and their radios crackled in their ears. 'Badger Squadron, this is Buttress. You are clear to land from the east. Wind at base level is twenty knots from the west.'

'Thank you, Buttress.'

Gwen lost sight of the entrance into the base for a few seconds as the three aircraft banked back on themselves, so as to approach from the Mediterranean side, but when she glanced back at it the door had already slid to a halt, fully open.

She eyed the hole apprehensively. 'Are we really supposed to fly into that?'

It wasn't that the entrance into the mountainside was small, because it very obviously wasn't, it was more that the act of flying into the side of a mountain seemed rather, well, *unnatural*.

'Don't worry, Goosy; that bloody hole's far bigger than the one the Prussians have to fly through to get on Bertha, and if those blighters can do it...'

'Then even *you* can, right, Digger?' Gwen interrupted, grinning across at Lion and its two occupants.

'Touché!'

The closer they got to the mountain, the more Gwen realised she was being silly worrying - the entry looked big enough to fly Buckingham Palace in. Minus the Brunel Tower, of course.

The Misfits landed in quick succession and were directed towards the hangar nearest the entrance.

Gwen handed Excalibur over into the care of a team of fitters, then gazed around the base as she stretched her legs. Hummingbird was there, as was a mountain of crates, which Gwen assumed contained the disassembled Dreadnought and Vulture - packed away because they were supposed to have been transferred to the Arturo as it passed. Apart from that the hangar was completely empty, but the next one down, separated from it by only a few extremely thick columns, was a hive of activity. Fitters were swarming all over a couple of squadron's worth of Spitsteams and there was a large group of pilots standing by in flight gear, as if ready to takeoff. Despite all the bustle and noise, none of the men and women working on the spotless and gleaming fighters actually seemed to be doing much of anything. The lights were off in the hangar beyond that and the weak daylight coming through the open door didn't reach, but she could just about make out some bombers, which looked like Nelsons, in it. There was nobody working on them, though, no pilots standing by, and for some reason she got the impression that they hadn't been flown for a while.

'I would have thought *someone* would come and greet us.' Abby said as Drake and Gwen joined her, raising her eyebrow at the Spitsteam pilots.

'Maybe they're intimidated by our Misfity-ness.' Drake grinned and waved cheerfully at the Spitsteam pilots. About half of them returned it automatically, proving they had been watching the Misfits surreptitiously.

'Here comes someone now.' Gwen inclined her head towards an officer, running towards them down the taxiway alongside the runway. He had greying hair, a waxed moustache of the style that was popular among RAC officers of a certain age for some reason, and was wearing a long great coat against the chill in the hangar. He paused to call out something to the fitters and pilots around the Spitsteams, waving at them urgently, before continuing to the Misfits. He skidded to a halt in front of them and spoke rapidly, somewhat out of breath, gesticulating wildly for them to follow him.

'The hangar door mechanism's jammed! We need everyone to help close it manually!'

'Can't it just stay open until it's repaired?' asked Tanya as the Misfits joined him and the rest of the Gibraltar base personnel in racing for the door.

The man shook his head. 'The Prussians watch the mountain. Every time the doors open they send a raid over from Tangiers, hoping to catch us with our trousers down. Their base is only thirty miles away - we only have five minutes to get them closed!'

Gwen looked around as she waddled along. None of the men and women seemed overly bothered by the door getting stuck, so it was probably something that happened regularly and had an easy solution.

Several people were already at the door, to one side of it at the end of the taxiway, slotting long metal poles into the holes in a black metal capstan, and the group found places on one of them as they arrived. Gwen found herself next to Drake and Tanya and together they leaned on the pole.

Drake grinned at Tanya. 'This is rather familiar.'

She just swore at him in Russian and bent to the task.

'Heave! Come on, put your backs into it! The Prussians are probably already half-way here by now!' The man who'd come running had jumped up onto the capstan and he shouted encouragement at them.

Gwen strained at the bar, but, despite the efforts of the dozens of men and women, it wasn't budging an inch. She pushed harder, her body almost horizontal, but still nothing happened. She refused to give up, though; they hadn't escaped the destruction of the Arturo just to have their machines destroyed by a faulty door in Gibraltar.

Slowly she became aware of the sounds around her. The grunts and groans of effort coming from the Misfits were the only ones she could hear. And was that a snigger?

She lifted her head and found that the four Misfits were the only ones pushing, everyone else was just leaning on the bars, watching them, wide smiles on their faces. She stood up straight, releasing the bar, and nudged Drake.

'What?' he asked, the strain evident in his voice.

'I think you can stop pushing now,' she said, then raised her voice. 'Abby, Tanya, we've been had.'

The other two Misfits lifted their own heads and looked around.

Abby scowled. 'What the devil? What's going on here?'

'Just a harmless little joke, Group Captain.' The man on the capstan crouched down so that he was more on their level. He was in his fifties, his face browned by the sun and creased with laughter lines, his hair perfectly in place despite the run across the base and coiffed in a style that had been popular with pilots during the First Great War. 'We do the same to anyone who lands for the first time, no matter the rank or service. We like to see if the people who arrive have a sense of humour, you see, Darwin knows you need one to stay sane in this place! And also *I* like to find out if they're willing to pitch in if needed or whether they'll only lift a finger at an order from a superior officer.' He fingered the cuff of his greatcoat, which bore no rank insignia, and looked at her expectantly.

Abby stared at him for a good few seconds, milking the moment, but then grinned. 'Well, it was a hell of a lot warmer and drier than what they did to us on the Arturo.' She pointed at the door. 'But the Prussians...?'

He grinned. 'Never fear, my dear! The Prussians aren't coming! Oh, they used to try to raid us all the time, but they stopped when they realised they were losing a hell of a lot of machines to our anti-aircraft guns and weren't doing anything except trimming the bushes and killing a few monkeys. Just in case, though,' he raised his voice and called out over his shoulder without looking. 'Corporal! Will you do the honours?'

'Sir!' A woman was standing ready at a small metal wheel protruding from the rock wall next to the open doorway. She casually, and without any apparent effort, began to turn it and the huge metal door smoothly and silently began to lower back into place.

'Wonderful engineering, what?' The man standing on the capstan jumped down and removed his greatcoat to reveal a day uniform of a style that had been retired more than twenty years before, with a long tunic and jodhpurs, but which bore the fairly recently redesigned rank insignia of a Sky Vice-Marshal. 'Welcome to RAC Gibraltar, I'm Bob Higgins and I run this blasted show.'

'Abby Lennox. And these are Gwen Stone, Rudy Drake and Tanya Guseva.'

'Pleased to meet you all.' He nodded at them. 'Let's go and get you some breakfast and then I'll take you on the tuppeny tour.'

Unlike the wonderfully elaborate and picturesque messes in the underground bases of Malta, the one in the mountain base was almost purely functional. Some effort had been made to make it look a little less like a hole in the rock, but there was only so much a lick of paint, a carpet and some plants could do. The food looked good, though, and the Misfits took full plates to one of the long wooden tables and tucked in to a full English breakfast with gusto.

Higgins had seen their expressions as they took in the mess and shrugged. 'It's not like anybody spends much time in here. There's accommodation for a few thousand people on the base, but we don't use it. Everyone lives in the town and there's another mess down there for all three services - the only people who ever eat in here are the ones on duty.'

'Nobody lives up here?'

'A few people do, mostly those men and women who use the workshops and design rooms for their own projects in their time off. You know the type - people who prefer to work on bringing their dreams to life instead of, well, dreaming.'

'Yes,' said Abby, glancing at Gwen, 'I know the type.'

Gwen scowled at her playfully. 'I'm not as bad as I used to be.'

'No, she's not,' Drake said to Higgins. 'I remember as a girl she used to turn up to flying lessons looking absolutely horrendous, with these horrible black bags under her eyes because she'd been in her workshop all night.' He grinned at Gwen. 'She's got an excuse to spend more time in bed *now*, though.'

'Well, I *did*.' Gwen snapped. She pushed her chair back from the table. 'I need more tea. Anyone want more tea?' She stalked off without waiting for an answer, though.

'Sorry, Gwen!'

Drake called after her, but Gwen didn't seem to hear, or was ignoring him.

Higgins gave Abby a questioning look and she sighed.

'Gwen is in a relationship with another of my pilots who was badly injured on the final day of fighting and had to be left behind.'

'Oh, that's rotten luck.'

'She might make it out, though. The hospital was built on a tunnel system and has been using them as wards. When we evacuated, the building was collapsed on top of those patients who couldn't be moved and the doctors who stayed to take care of them. The tunnels connect with the sea and we were told the navy would try to get them out by undersea boat, but it's enemy territory now and it might be too risky to even attempt.'

'I know how it feels to leave people behind,' Higgins said sadly. 'I had to leave a lot of good men and women behind in France.'

Abby grimaced. 'You and me both. But to have to leave a lover...' She sighed. 'I guess we just have to wait and see what the navy can do. By the way, do you know what's happening with the Arturo?'

The Misfits had been getting regular updates on the rescue efforts dispatched from Gibraltar while they had been in the air and had heard that two frigates, a destroyer, and a dozen fast launches had been sent to the scene of the attack - the war ships to help track down the Prussian undersea boat and the launches to pick up the survivors, or at least tow lifeboats back to Gibraltar. They had landed before the boats had reached the Arturo's last known position, though, and hadn't heard how many survivors there had been, or even whether the ship had actually sunk in the end.

'I don't, sorry, but we'll pop into the comms room and find out as soon as you've finished.'

Gwen stared at the huge brass tea urn, clutching her freshly-filled metal mug, oblivious to the burning sensation in her hand.

It had been a whole eight hours since she'd gotten into bed and taken a last look at the photograph she kept with her always. A whole eight hours that she hadn't thought about Kitty and the very distinct possibility that she would never see her again. A whole eight hours during which she'd either been asleep or too busy or terrified to think of anything except what she was doing.

But then Drake had to go and burst that very flimsy bubble she'd been walking around in and bring all her doubts and fears flooding back.

It had been a very lonely, very fretful four days since they'd left Malta and Kitty behind. The daylight hours were bad, but she'd managed to keep her mind occupied with the repairs to Excalibur. The nights had been much worse, though; a never ending procession of nightmares, until she'd been too tired to stay awake, but too scared to sleep. The evening before the attack she'd finally turned to drink in an effort to dull her senses and help her sleep, going to a mess on the opposite side of the ship so that the Misfits wouldn't walk in on her. It had worked, after a fashion - the time had passed quicker and the nightmares hadn't been as overwhelming - but it had only been a temporary solution and it wasn't something she could do every night.

Everyone kept telling her that she didn't have to be so worried, that Kitty would be fine, but she just couldn't see how. The plan to get her out was risky to say the least. So many things could go wrong with it - the undersea boat could be spotted coming and give away that the British were there, or worse, destroyed once it had picked them up! And that was without taking into consideration that the Prussians might find the tunnels on their own before Kitty was well enough to travel and she could end up in Gruber's hands.

The thought of him putting her to work in the winding room of Bertha, like he had Rudy, was one of those things that most fuelled her nightmares and she found herself getting lost in a vision of Kitty wasting away at a capstan, which was now very much like the one in the hangar just a few hundred yards away.

'Y'alright, ma'am?'

Gwen started and looked up, blinking away tears she hadn't felt coming, and became aware of one of the white-coated cooks standing next to her, peering at her in concern.

'Yes, thank you. I, uh... I just swallowed the wrong way.'

She forced a smile, then turned away and went back to her friends.

The Misfits polished off their food quickly, eager to hear what was happening to the Arturo and their friends aboard her.

The news was tragic, but hopeful. The Arturo had still been afloat, barely, the fires all but put out by the encroaching sea, when the naval vessels had rendezvoused with her. They had been able to evacuate far more of the crew than would have survived otherwise, including Captain Hewer, who insisted that everyone left alive was off his ship before abandoning it himself. The warships, including the two which had been escorting the Arturo, were still hunting the Prussian undersea boat, but the launches had begun to make their painfully slow way back to Gibraltar, each with dozens of lifeboats in tow. It would be hours before they reached safety, so Higgins asked the officer in charge to send someone to inform him if there was any news, then led the pilots back out.

The next stop was the hangar next to the one the Misfits had been assigned, where the two Spitsteam squadrons, 202 and 204 squadrons, were berthed. 202 squadron was getting ready to go on a patrol, but their leader, who was also in overall command of the fighter squadrons, took the time to meet them.

Justine Charmers was thirty-six, with greying blonde hair and a deeply lined face, especially around her startlingly-light blue eyes. She had joined the RAC eight years after the end of the First Great War, straight out of unniversity. At first she had met the same kind of resistance and prejudice as Dorothy Campbell and had advanced very slowly through the ranks, only making squadron leader while almost all of her male contemporaries were at least group captains, if not commodores or marshals. Then, when war had broken out, she'd been sent away to take command of the fighters at Gibraltar, the thinking apparently being that the peninsula was impregnable and that it wouldn't matter if the two squadrons were commanded by a woman. Thankfully, that kind of attitude had been extinguished extremely quickly when the female pilots of the RAC had demonstrated themselves to be just as competent as the male pilots during the Battle over Britain. It didn't hurt that fully half of Misfit Squadron, including their two most famous pilots, Gwen and Abby, were female, either. Unfortunately, that didn't help her very much in Gibraltar and she was stuck there with no relief in sight and not very much to do, with the Prussians not having attacked in months. She seemed cheerful enough, though, and greeted the Misfits warmly, even going so far as inviting them to fly with her squadron whenever they liked.

They stayed to watch the Spitsteams take off out of professional interest, taking note of how they were able to use the width of the runway to get all twelve aircraft out of the west side of the mountain already formed in their elements and in extremely quick order, but then continued the tour by continuing along to the hangar they'd been assigned. They were pleased to see that their aircraft were being well taken care of by the obviously competent fitters and were more than happy to leave them to it and allow Higgins to show them the rooms adjoining the hangar, which were now theirs. There was a ready room that was easily big enough for half a dozen fighter squadrons or more. A work crew was in the process of cleaning and setting up the room for them, bringing in a tea urn and a table for food and removing dust covers to reveal matching sofas and armchairs which looked like they'd never been used. Through a door to one side was a large changing room and attached to that was a bathroom, with a dozen toilet stalls and what looked like enough showers for a regiment to bathe together.

There wasn't very much to see, so Higgins moved on quickly, taking them back towards the mess, along the wide footpath which ran the length of the base between the hangars and the other rooms. They had a quick peek through a couple of the doors they came across into a design room and a small workshop, both of which were in use by a surprising amount of people, but they didn't bother going down any of the short corridors that led to things like the armoury, the briefing room and the offices.

The living quarters Higgins had mentioned were down a moderately wide corridor near the centre of the runway, next to the mess, but he just waved vaguely at it, said "barracks" and didn't stop.

They looked into the third hangar as they went past, where the bombers indeed proved to be Pickford Nelsons, as Gwen had thought. There were twenty-four of them, comprising two squadrons - 148 and 223 - and they were dusty from disuse. Higgins insisted they were in tip-top condition and ready to fly at a moment's notice, though, and pointed out two groups of mechanics were carrying out routine maintenance on a couple of the machines.

The fourth hangar was dark and empty and they barely glanced at it as they kept walking. Higgins pointed out another workshop and a machine shop for making ammunition, as well as the corridors which led to the generator, the water pump and the various spaces for food storage, but then they were at the end of the footpath. The tour ended there, at the far west end of the base, where the lifts that went from the town below, all the way up to the summit of the Rock, were situated. There were five in total, an extremely large one for freight, and four smaller ones, which were still far larger than normal lifts and carried up to thirty passengers each. Scarlet, Derek, Wendy and Owen were waiting for them there, polishing off a large plate of bacon sandwiches between them. Bruce was there too, but he was sitting to one side, against the wall by one of the passenger lifts, cradling a steaming mug. He looked a bit paler than he had before takeoff and Abby frowned at him before looking to Scarlet. 'Is he alright?'

She nodded. 'I got the Medics to check him out as soon as we arrived. He's fine. He just got a bit cold on the journey.'

'Good, thank you,' Abby said. She looked around the small group. 'Why didn't you come and find us?'

'We had the tour days ago.' Owen said, his arm around Wendy. 'And besides.' He waved the remains of his sandwich at her as an explanation, before stuffing it in his mouth.

'And I couldn't be bothered to wander around,' Scarlet said with a mischievous grin. 'I'll explore in my own way later.'

Abby rolled her eyes and looked sideways at Higgins. She jerked her thumb over her shoulder at a couple of very bored-looking military guards on duty next to the lifts. 'Please ask your MG's not to shoot any short Irishwomen they find sneaking around the base please.'

'Don't worry, Abby, they'll never see me.'

Higgins looked at Scarlet with new interest. 'Care to make a wager?'

'That wouldn't be fair on you.'

'Really?' Higgins grinned eagerly. 'What odds will you give me, then?'

Abby shook her head in exasperation. 'It's quite boring here, isn't it?'

'Whatever gave you that idea?' Higgins replied with a laugh, but immediately turned back to Scarlet. However, before he could start haggling with her over exact terms of their wager, there was a sweet-sounding ping and the door to the lift on the far left slid open. Scarlet and Derek helped Bruce up and they all followed the base commander into it.

In stark contrast to the base, which was more akin to a cave than anything else - all bare rock and metal, with only a few attempts at homeliness in the more frequented areas - the lift was like something which belonged more in a luxury apartment building in London, or one of the more exclusive department stores. It had a mahogany floor, dark green wallpaper with a gold pattern and electric sconce lamps with glass shades in the middle of each wall instead of the usual bright overhead lighting. A brass panel by the door held buttons for the three floors the lift stopped at, with "0", "1" and "2" engraved next to them in an elegant script. Simple plaques made from thin sheets of Duralumin, which in no way matched the style of the rest of the lift, had been fixed next to them. They were also engraved, but with cheeky alternatives to the simple numbers.

The top one read "Heaven", the middle one read "Hell" and the bottom one "Purgatory".

Higgins grinned, but pushed the one labelled "Heaven" without comment. The doors closed with another ping and the lift accelerated upwards smoothly.

Owen looked at the newly arrived pilots. 'So, did you fall for the capstan thing?'

Abby grimaced as she nodded. 'Yes. Did they do that to you too?'

'They tried.' Owen smirked at Higgins. 'But Wendy took one look at the capstan and realised it was a fake. She just pushed everyone out of the way and turned that wheel on the wall.'

'That wasn't all she did,' said Higgins with a laugh. 'I've never seen anyone make such a rude-looking gesture!'

Scarlet's eyes widened as she turned to Wendy. 'You gave them the old...?' She tilted her head to one side, clicked her tongue twice, then whistled and flapped an elbow.

Wendy nodded. 'I did.'

'Wow, I'm so jealous,' the Irishwoman shook her head. 'I've never had the opportunity to use that one.'

Owen glanced back and forth between the two women and frowned. 'What else have you been teaching my wife?'

'Wouldn't you like to know?' Scarlet winked at him. 'Word of advice, though, don't ever rub her up the wrong way.'

Owen's frown deepened as much as it could in his burn-ravaged face, but before he could quiz her further, the doors opened.

Only two of the passenger lifts went all the way up to the top of the Rock and the cargo lift had its own unloading dock and exit to the mountainside so the lobby beyond was very small. They followed Higgins across it, then through a thick door, down a short tunnel, through another very thick door, before finally going up a short flight of stairs and into blinding sunshine.

'Gosh.'

'Gosh, indeed,' said Drake, agreeing with Gwen's comment.

They were on the north side of the flat concrete platform at the very summit of the Rock, almost fourteen hundred feet up, with Spain in front of them. To their left they could see across the bay all the way to the Spanish town of Algeciras, only five miles away, while to their right was the open sea, sparkling in the morning sunlight.

The view was breathtaking, even for pilots who were used to impressive views, however, that wasn't what Higgins had brought them up to look at - it was the guns that liberally studded the mountaintop they had come to see.

The platform had originally been constructed in 1915 to hold the two massive guns which formed the backbone of the isolated British territory's defence. "Victoria" and "Victor", as they were fondly known, had been state of the art when they'd been made and were still unmatched in all the world. Based on a set of sketches Brunel had made a couple of years before he'd died, they were unique, not just for their size or their long range, but also because of their nature. Huge steam engines, even now sending barely perceptible vibrations through the rock as they idled in constant readiness, were ensconced in a chamber hewn from the rock of the mountain directly below them. These not only moved the immensely heavy shells up from the silo and directly into their breeches, but also powered them, compressing air in the steel-bound chambers at the rear of the guns to incredible pressures so as to fling the tons of metal all the way to Africa or far into Spain.

As time had gone by, more and more guns emplacements had been constructed on the mountain until now there were a few dozen other artillery pieces. Those guns looked tiny in comparison to the two that dominated the summit, but were in fact among the heaviest guns in regular production, able to easily reach the far side of the isthmus to the north, which was the only way into Gibraltar by land, or bombard any ships that dared get too close. Paths led off from the platform in all directions to an additional fifty anti-aircraft gun emplacements, all with nearly uninterrupted lines of sight. Large searchlights also dotted the landscape, as did various radar and radio towers, and there was a slightly lower plateau directly in front of them with more guns and antenna. All in all, there was as much firepower on the mountain as there had been around Valletta, for example, and that was without counting the dozens more guns around its base, along the defensive wall, and throughout the docks, or taking into consideration the advantage the height at which the guns were positioned gave them.

Higgins held out his arms, as if he were a circus ringmaster presenting his acts, and raised his voice to be heard over the wind. 'This, ladies and gentlemen, is why, as your commander so astutely put it, things are "quite boring" here.' He turned in place and began gesturing grandly out at the landscape. 'We hold an unassailable position here on our little peninsula. An approach from the sea is impossible. Not only is that fleet sitting down there, aching to blow apart any Prussian that sails this way, but one hit from a "Vic" will sink even one of their biggest battleships. If they decide to come by air, we have so many anti-aircraft batteries that most of their bombers will be knocked out of the sky before they get close enough to drop their bombs and any that do survive will be mopped up by the Spits. And as for an assault from the land, well, that would just be stupid. Not only do we have a few dozen bombers, but we have all this artillery, which will pound them to bits while they're still miles away! Not that the Spanish would ever allow the Prussians to march an army hundreds of miles through their territory anyway!'

He finally dropped his arms to his sides. 'The Prussians know all that - they had enough of an opportunity to pay Gibraltar a visit between the wars and inspect our defences because the bloody mayor invited them! They're *fully* aware that this bloody great stone isn't worth what it would cost to try to take it from us and they're not bothering to properly threaten us or do anything much to stop our activities. They've got a token few squadrons of aircraft in Tangiers, along with a couple of divisions of troops, but the nearest real force of any kind is in France.'

He grinned at Abby, then winked at Scarlet. 'So, with the civilians all evacuated and nothing to do apart from keep a watch out for an attack that will never come, do you blame us for trying to find any amusement we can?'

He pushed himself away from the rail and started towards the other side of the plateau. 'Let's go and have a look at Africa, shall we?'

A path, about five yards wide and a hundred long, its edges marked with yellow paint, had been left clear down the middle of the concrete platform, between the rotating platforms holding the enormous guns. The Misfits followed Higgins along it all the way to the southern end of the platform, from where they could see clear to Africa.

'The straight is about a dozen miles wide here, but Tangiers is over there, a bit more than thirty-five miles away.' Higgins pointed a bit to the right of the closest land they could see. 'That's where the Prussians have those aircraft and troops and it's where an attack would come from.'

'But with what you've told us about the defences, would they ever attack?' asked Abby.

Higgins shrugged. 'They might if the Prussians had a commander crazy or egotistical enough, or the Kaiser ordered them to. But if they wanted to have any kind of guarantee of success they would need to dedicate as many resources, if not more, than they did to try to take Britain last summer and they haven't got nearly enough free. Not even if they brought in everything they threw against you in Malta.'

The pilots stared across at the other continent, but there was not a lot to see, no sign of the Prussian aircraft the vice-marshal said were there, not even through the lenses of their helmets so when he suggested they go back to the base a few minutes later they agreed readily.

Instead of going back the way they'd come, Higgins took them around the west side of the platform so that they could take a quick look down into the town and harbour as they went.

Aside from there being dozens of warships in the port and the bay beyond, there was almost no sign that the war had come to Gibraltar. The terraced houses, mansions and warehouses covering the slopes of the foot of the mountain were completely intact. There were no bomb craters, no blackened and gutted buildings, instead the scene was almost peaceful, with quite a few people actually sunning themselves next to the water towards the southern end of the peninsula. It looked more like a British seaside resort than a fortress, and more than one of the pilots paused to take in the near-normality of the scene. However, it was quite cold in the shadow of the two big guns, especially with the wind off the sea whistling across the high plateau, so they didn't tarry too long and went to take the lift back down.

As soon as they stepped out onto the cool stone of the base Higgins turned to address them again. 'Well, ladies and gentlemen, that concludes our tour. If you've enjoyed yourself, please tell your friends and we hope to see you again soon!' He beamed while the Misfits laughed, but then turned serious, or at least as serious as he ever seemed to get. 'Things are going to get a bit busy when the survivors of the Arturo arrive so I'd recommend you get some uniforms from stores, which is right down *that* corridor,' he pointed at a corridor a few yards down from the cargo lift, 'then go and say hello to the port admiral at Navy Headquarters. I have to stay here, because I'm *supposed* to be on duty, but anyone in the town will be able to tell you where that is, unless your friend hasn't already broken in and stolen the admiral's rum...?'

He pointedly looked at Scarlet who grinned. 'Don't give me ideas.'

He returned her smile. 'We definitely have to talk about that wager. Drinks tonight?'

'As long as you're buying.'

'Of course! I'll come and get you at six.' He turned to Abby. 'We'll talk properly when you're settled in. Tomorrow? Say ten?'

'Yes, sir.'

'Excellent! Until then! Toodle-pip!' He nodded, then strolled off, whistling jauntily and calling out greetings to everyone he passed.

The Misfits watched him go, all rather bemused.

'What a strange man.' Tanya said.

CHAPTER 3

The uniforms that the Misfits who'd flown in that morning were issued from stores were brand new, smelled strongly of mothballs, were a bit dusty and creased after being folded up for months, and didn't fit them very well. They weren't nearly as presentable as they usually were, but going to see the port admiral, the highest ranked officer in overall command of Gibraltar, in coveralls wasn't an option, so it was either wear them or waddle around in flightsuits all day.

The Spitsteams were landing by the time they came back out of the ready rooms after changing and they watched them as they wandered back towards the lifts. The pilots didn't do nearly as impressive a job getting down as they had done taking off, with a few of them even bouncing a few times, making all of the Misfits, but especially Drake, who had been a flight instructor, wince.

'Just as well this lot won't have to fight the Prussians,' muttered Bruce rather unkindly, 'they'd be slaughtered.'

The rest of the pilots shot each other dismayed looks behind his back. While they were all thinking more or less the same thing, they would never say it out loud; it just wasn't done. They *weren't* particularly surprised by his tone, though. Ever since the death of his friend and wingman, Monty Fletcher, and his own brush with the Dark Scythesman during the mission to destroy the Barons' gigantic airship, Bertha, Bruce had become dour and pessimistic in sharp contrast to his previous clowning and perpetual good humour. They had hoped that he would recover once his injuries had healed enough for him to do things to take his mind off his woes, but he showed no sign of doing so and when he spoke, which wasn't often, it was usually only to offer some sarcastic or disparaging comment. The events of the morning hadn't exactly helped either, especially because what few keepsakes he and any of them had of Monty and the other lost Misfits had gone down with the Arturo, along with most of their personal items.

Navy Headquarters, where the port admiral, Rear Admiral Sir Rodney Tipperton, had his offices, weren't down by the harbour, as they'd naturally expected, but rather the pilots were pointed towards a luxurious mansion on the lower slopes of the mountain not far from the Moorish Castle. They had been moved from the large building on the waterfront, which they had occupied since the eighteenth century, in order to not present such an easy target for Prussian bombers and so that the senior officers could be quickly evacuated into the mountain if necessary.

The three-storey house was set back from a street in its own fenced off compound, surrounded by a garden, which was starting to get rather overgrown. There were no guards on the street outside the open gate, nor were there any at the door, which was also open wide, and the Misfits were able to just walk straight in unchallenged.

A small wooden desk had been set up to one side, just inside the entrance, in what had once been an impressive hallway with marble tiles on the wide floor in a chessboard pattern and portraits on the maroon walls. A young seaman was sitting behind it, bent over a newspaper, his head propped up in his hands.

'Yes? What can I...?' He looked up from his reading and came to an abrupt, wide-eyed halt when he saw the group of RAC officers gathered around his desk, most of them watching him in amusement. 'Blimey!' He hurriedly tore the paper off the desk and stuffed it into a drawer before shooting out of his chair, almost knocking it over, and standing to attention.

'Morning, Seaman.' Abby said, smiling at him reassuringly. 'We're here to see the admiral. Would you let him know we're here, please? I'm afraid we don't have an appointment.'

'That's alright, ma'am, uh Group... uh... Dame Lennox, I'll go and... I... I'll...' Realising what a mess he was making of things, the sailor turned bright red and scampered off towards the back of the house and through a door to the side.

'Do you think he recognised us?' asked Scarlet.

Less than twenty seconds later the sailor reappeared and ran back to them. 'Uh, if you would come with me, please, ma'am?'

There was a door to one side of his desk and he opened it for them to reveal a spacious lounge area. 'If you'd kindly wait here, someone will be with you as soon as possible.'

Abby nodded at him, giving him another warm smile. 'Thank you.'

He smiled at her and bobbed his head nervously, then went back to his desk, leaving the door open.

While most of the pilots either flopped into the armchairs or made a beeline for a table holding a tea urn and biscuits, Derek moved towards a pile of newspapers on a sideboard and began flicking through them.

'Anything interesting, Derek?' Abby called out as Scarlet poured tea in a cup for her.

'Just the usual stuff from home. "We're taking a beating, but Britain battles on!" that kind of...' he paused and ripped a smaller paper from the pile. 'What the hell is this?' He stalked over to the others, brandishing what he'd found. 'Do any of you know about this?'

He slammed the paper down on the buffet table, almost knocking over a plate of biscuits, then smoothed out the damage that had been caused by his rough treatment of it before stepping back to let the others see.

'*Misfit Monthly. The adventures and misadventures of Britain's most famed pilots.*' Drake read. 'Sounds promising.'

Abby tapped the top corner of the cover. 'This was published in March and apparently it's only the second issue, which explains why we've never seen it before.'

The paper was slightly smaller than a tabloid newspaper and quite thin, with less than thirty pages. The cover was in colour, with an aircraft, recognisably Excalibur, although many of the details were wrong, seen head on in the foreground. She was being pursued by two red aircraft, which had lines of bright yellow fire spouting from their wings and streaming past her. At the bottom of the page was a title in large, bright red writing - *Gwen Stone Ambushed!*

'Ooh!' said Scarlet. 'Am I in it?'

Abby began turning the pages. It was mostly writing inside, set out in three columns, stories by the look of them, each one capped by a small black and white picture that probably represented the contents.

Drake chortled when Abby got to the middle of the paper. 'Looks like it!'

There was another colour drawing, this one taking up the entirety of the centre pages - a rather amateurish rendering of Hummingbird, with a waving, rather scantily clad and far more detailed Scarlet perched half out of the cockpit.

The Irishwoman cooed in appreciation. 'I want a copy of that!'

It was fairly clear that the picture was on the centre pages precisely so that it could be removed and she reached out and started picking at the staples, but Abby batted her hand away.

'This isn't ours. You'll have to find your own.'

While Scarlet pouted, Abby kept going. So far there hadn't been anything too offensive - even the drawing of Scarlet had been tasteful up to a point - but there was still fully half of the thing to go.

The page immediately after the centre had a cartoon strip titled "Hapless Hans", which depicted Gruber as an evil, but bumbling character. Abby paused briefly so that everyone could read it, but nobody found it particularly funny and she moved on. There were more stories after that and she scanned each without stopping; they were just more of the usual exaggerations or fabrications that filled the tabloids on a daily basis and not really worthy of reading. It wasn't until she got to the very last story, or more precisely the picture that introduced it, that she found something that caught her attention. The picture was larger than most of the others, with more care and artistic talent put into it and depicted a vaguely familiar woman leaning back in the arms of a handsome man, about to share a kiss.

Drake laughed and leaned close. 'I think that's supposed to be you, Goosy!' He put his finger on the text. 'Look at this!'

Gwen peered at the writing and groaned.

Drake put on a breathy voice and began to read. '"Gwen's hand drifted down his hard chest as she leaned in to whisper in his ear, her voice purring like Excalibur's airscrew..."'

'Oh for...!' Gwen interrupted in disgust, 'who writes this drivel?'

'More to the point, who reads it?' asked Derek, just as offended as she was.

'It's actually quite popular.'

The Misfits looked up to find a female Navy officer in the doorway, a commander with greying blonde hair pulled back into a tight bun and a deeply lined face.

'The first issue of Misfit Monthly had a print run of a hundred thousand and sold out in a matter of hours apparently. A million copies were printed for the second and it sold out in less than two days. I've heard they printed even more for the third and fourth.'

'We should ask for royalties, then,' said Scarlet.

'Perhaps you should.' The woman nodded earnestly. 'As for who writes it - look at the back.'

Gwen pushed Drake out of the way and closed the paper quickly, hiding the offending article before he could finish reading it. The back cover was taken up in its entirety by a familiar image, one of the many propaganda posters that the War Ministry had produced over the previous year, this one urging the populace to donate any spare copper they might have. *Help our boys and girls FIGHT! Put a SPRING in their step... and their autocar, and their aircraft!* At the bottom of the page, though, was a very small footnote.

'Printed and published by The Spoke,' she read, 'with the kind permission of the War Ministry.'

Derek sighed. 'Figures that it would be The Spoke; they're the worst kind of tabloid.'

'But the War Ministry? Why would they give permission for this... this...?' Gwen held the paper up between forefinger and thumb, wrinkling her nose as if at a bad smell.

'Well, that's obvious too,' Derek said. 'It is merely a continuation of Cummerbund's war against us and the King himself. He's seeking to ridicule us and therefore undermine him.'

There was a moment of silence as the pilots evaluated Derek's assessment of the paper's true purpose, but then Scarlet laughed. 'Nah! The Misfits sell papers and Cummerbund is probably getting a cut - he'll be making money hand over fist from us!'

Scarlet seized the paper and opened it up to the centre pages, but Abby took it from her before she could remove the picture and handed it to Derek who put it back with the other newspapers.

'I don't think we're going to get a proper answer to this until we get back to London and speak to the King,' the group captain said. 'For now, I prefer to think that the ministry is allowing this because it's another way of keeping up morale, rather than it being another attack.' Abby wasn't convinced that Derek's assessment wasn't correct, but she didn't want to continue the debate right then, especially not when there was an audience, so she put on a smile and turned to the forgotten naval officer. 'Sorry about that. We've been out of the loop for a while and the paper came as a bit of a surprise.'

'I understand completely.' The woman smiled and came forward with her hand extended. 'Dame Lennox, I'm Commander Bailey, one of the admiral's aides. Seaman Twist tells me you'd like to see him.'

Abby shook the hand. 'Yes, please.'

Bailey shook the hands of the pilots one by one before answering. 'I'm afraid the admiral is stuck in the communications office, waiting for a call from the War Minister. He apologises, but he won't be able to receive you at the moment. Did you need something urgently? Is there something I can help with?'

'It was just a courtesy call, to let him know we've landed in his lap and will get out of his hair as soon as possible.'

'Ah! I will let him know, but I'm sure he'll want to meet you himself when he has time, perhaps over tea or dinner in the next few days, after everyone from the Arturo has been seen to. I hope you'll understand he'll be busy until then.'

'Of course, but I don't know if we'll be around for that long; I'm sure we'll be continuing our journey as soon as we can.'

Bailey hesitated before replying and the smiles of more than one of the Misfits drooped when they realised that there was more bad news coming, to be piled on top of everything that had already gone wrong that day. 'The next convoy isn't due for a month and no ships will be leaving Gibraltar until then, so I'm afraid you're stuck with us for a while.'

She smiled apologetically at their long faces. 'I'm sorry, but in the meantime I hope you'll allow us to extend our hospitality to you. We have good food, good wine, good accommodation and, as you've no doubt already noticed, it's relatively quiet here. I know it's not an ideal situation, but if half of what I've heard about Malta is true, you could probably do with some rest. Maybe you could look on this as a month of paid leave?'

Abby looked around her pilots. With few exceptions, most notably Gwen, they had been keen to get home to friends and loved ones, but they seemed to be warming very quickly to the idea of having some time off.

She nodded reluctantly. 'That actually sounds quite good. *Although,*' she gave her squadron a hard look, 'we will *not* be taking a month off - we might rest for a few days *at some point*, but we're going to keep up on our training so that we're ready to get straight back into the war when we get home. Understood?'

She waited for acknowledgements, then turned back to Bailey. 'Well, I suppose we're going to need some of that lovely accommodation of yours, please.'

'Wonderful! Let's see if we can find you somewhere comfortable. Seaman!'

There was a rustle of paper and the thump of a drawer closing before the young man appeared in the doorway. 'Ma'am?'

'Run and get the accommodation list, would you, please?'

'Aye aye, ma'am.'

He disappeared instantly, his footsteps fading as he raced up the hallway outside, obeying her order as literally as he could.

'Do you mind?' Bailey pointed at the tea, 'I haven't had a chance for a break all morning and I'm parched.'

'Please.'

She moved towards the urn and the pilots stepped aside to make way for her.

The thunder of footsteps sounded from the hallway outside almost before she could finish pouring a cup, though, and she took a quick gulp before reluctantly setting it aside and going to accept a large blue folder from the seaman when he reappeared in the doorway. 'Thank you.'

'Ma'am.'

Bailey put the folder on the table next to the urn and began running a finger down the hand-written list that filled the first few pages in it.

'Ah, here we go.' She tapped an entry, then flicked through the thick wedge of papers until she found what she wanted. 'With all the civilians evacuated we've got plenty of room, even with all the people coming from the Arturo, so you can have a townhouse all to yourselves.' She made a note on a slip of paper, then handed it to Abby. 'Here's the address. It's not far from here.'

Owen leaned in to read the slip of paper. 'I know where that is. It's a few doors down from the temporary digs they put me and Wendy in.'

Abby nodded at the commander. 'Thank you.'

'You're welcome,' she said. She closed the folder and laid it to the side before picking up her cup again. 'Well, that's accommodation taken care of. As for food - you need to get hold of dress uniforms if you plan to go to the officer's mess and you'll need them for when you dine with Admiral Tipperton. You'll also want basic necessities. I'd recommend you go to stores down here rather than up in the RAC base for things like toothpaste and soap; you'll find it hasn't been in storage quite as long. And Royal Navy underwear is a hell of a lot softer than that scratchy stuff they force you Wreckers to wear!'

The pilots laughed and Abby smiled. 'That would be much appreciated.'

Bailey returned the smile warmly. 'Is there anything else I can do for you?'

'Actually, there is one more thing.'

'Yes?'

'The last report we had on the Arturo was over an hour ago, can you find out if there's anything more recent?'

'I was actually compiling the latest report for the admiral myself, just before I came to see you.' The commander said. 'The boats won't get into harbour for a while yet, but the hospital staff are even now preparing to meet them and we already have a rough count of the number of survivors - it looks like almost ninety percent have been saved, which is remarkable for this kind of attack. We'll compile a list as soon as we can and post it on all the noticeboards around town, but with all the chaos of the evacuation and then the attack we might never know exactly who went down with the Arturo.'

There wasn't much more to say, so, after making sure that there was nothing else that they needed, Bailey took her leave of them and the Misfits went back out into the hallway. Before they left, though, Abby went back up to the desk and loomed over the young man.

'Seaman Twist, isn't it?'

He swallowed and looked up at her nervously. 'Yes, ma'am?'

'Get it out, Seaman.'

'Ma'am?' His eyebrows shot up in alarm.

She pointed down, behind the desk. 'That *thing* you have in the drawer. Get it out.'

Twist turned bright red once more as he reluctantly pulled what he'd been reading from the drawer - a copy of Misfit Monthly - and laid it on the desk in front of her.

Abby tutted and shook her head. 'This just won't do; it isn't right.' She stared coldly at him. 'Do you have a pen?'

'A pen? Uh, yes, ma'am. Here.'

He handed her a dark blue, Royal Navy issue pen and she held it poised above the paper. The young man winced, sure that she was about to "correct" or deface it in some way, but instead she leaned down and signed the cover. She finished with a flourish and waved the pen at him in admonishment. 'This is in no way an endorsement of the rubbish printed in here, understood?'

'Yes, ma'am!' the grinning man answered.

Abby nodded, gave him a grin, then passed the pen to the next pilot, Scarlet, who immediately opened the paper to the centre pages.

With nothing much else to do and lunch only an hour or so away, the Misfits decided to go and take a look at their house and drop off what few personal items they'd been able to bring from the Arturo.

'What are we supposed to do for a month?' asked Drake.

'Maybe they'll let us build new aircraft,' said Derek, an eager gleam in his eye.

Abby shrugged. 'I doubt they can spare the resources. That doesn't mean you can't work on designs in those lovely design rooms they have, though.'

'Actually,' said Wendy, 'I've already had a look around their workshops and they have plenty of resources to spare; they have so little to do that they haven't been using anything and every convoy just brings more. I'm going to ask for some space to work while I'm here and I'm sure the fitters on the base will be glad for something interesting to do instead of twiddling their thumbs all day.'

Abby nodded. 'Alright, I'll talk to Higgins when I see him tomorrow, but don't get your hopes up too much. Unlike the scrap we got from the Graveyard on Malta, the materials on the base all belong to the RAC. Remember that lovely little message from the War Minister telling us we couldn't rebuild?'

'How could we forget? But do you think Higgins will know about it?'

Silence greeted Owen's question, but after a few seconds Scarlet started to laugh. 'Ooh, devious! I like it!'

The rest of the pilots joined in and even Bruce chuckled half-heartedly for a couple of seconds.

Gwen didn't. After the excitement of the morning had finished it had been so easy to slip back into misery and loneliness, especially after Drake's thoughtless comment, and she was lagging a few paces behind the group, lost in her thoughts, barely looking at the surroundings and not participating in the conversation or even really listening to it. She had been the same during the tour of the base and when Higgins had taken them up to the summit and expounded on the invulnerability of Gibraltar she had wandered off on her own and gazed out over the Mediterranean to the east, towards Malta and Kitty.

She'd been aware of Drake watching her during that time and had been very glad that he was leaving her alone, not in the mood for his joking, or the half-arsed apology she knew he would try to make at some point.

Here he came now, though...

That look was back on Gwen's face. She'd had it for the last few days. Ever since they'd landed on the Arturo after leaving Malta. Ever since the reality of leaving Kitty behind had hit her full force and she'd realised just how much of a chance there was that she'd never see her again. He'd heard her moaning in her sleep and smelled the alcohol on her breath when she'd come stumbling home around midnight, bumping into the beds and grumbling angrily.

The one consolation was that it wasn't as bad as the look she'd had on her face every so often in Muscovy. According to Scarlet and Kitty, Gwen was throwing herself into fights without much thought for self-preservation back then, after the death of her husband, Richard. He could be fairly sure that she wouldn't do anything silly, right then, though, at least not unless news came of Kitty falling into enemy hands. Or worse.

It was only a small consolation, though, because the squadron's morale was already low enough without Bruce and Gwen walking around as if they were teetotallers in a pub and that could get them, and others, killed.

She *had* to be brought out of her melancholy somehow, if not for her sake then everyone else's, so he dropped back to walk beside her, determined to try.

'You've been awfully quiet today, Gwen. I would have thought you'd at least have said *something* after we went through the design room and saw that boy drawing a flying battleship with sails and everything. I mean, I *know* he was probably doing it for fun or an art project, rather than trying to create something practical, but you must admit his designs were pretty funny.'

Apparently, Higgins had organised a kind of unofficial university in Gibraltar, roping in dozens of volunteers to teach classes in whatever they had some knowledge of, both to fill the time for bored servicemen and women and to give them an opportunity to improve themselves. There had been a class going on in the large design room that Higgins had taken them through on the tour - one of the RAC officers had a degree from the University of Merthyr Tydfil in aeronautics and was teaching a course in aircraft design to those men and women interested, or bored, enough to take it. There had been about fifteen people of varying ages there, a few of them Royal Navy personnel and the young Airman in question couldn't have been more than eighteen. He had been intently filling a large sheet of paper with one sketch after another, each more fantastic than the last, none of which would rise even an inch off the ground.

Gwen chuckled in reply, but her heart obviously wasn't in it and she still didn't comment.

Drake grimaced. For her not to rise to such an obvious bait about aircraft design meant things were even worse than he'd thought.

'Look, I'm sorry about before in the mess. I spoke before thinking. You know me - I tend to do that a lot.'

'Don't worry about it.'

The reply was flat, with barely any emotion and Drake's frown deepened.

'You know she'll be...'

'*Don't* say it.'

Drake was brought up in his tracks, startled into silence, at Gwen's sudden vehemence as she all but shouted at him.

She stopped walking too and turned to glare at him. 'I'm sick and bloody tired of everyone saying that Kitty will be fine! You don't know that! *Anything* could happen to her between Malta and here. Just look what happened to *us*!'

Drake didn't back away in the face of her anger, instead he stepped in and wrapped his arms tightly around her. 'She *will* be fine, Gwen. She's been through a lot worse in her time and has more to fight for now. The Navy will get her out and she'll be here before you know it.' He gave her a squeeze, then pulled back to arm's length and smiled warmly. 'Who knows, she might even get here before we catch the next convoy.'

Gwen snarled at Rudy for his unwanted familiarity and started to shrug his hands off her shoulders. She stopped, though, when she realised that what he was saying did actually make perfect sense. Kitty was a survivor. She had made it through the Iberian Civil War, getting out not only with her life, but her aircraft as well, while the rest of her squadron perished. She had even been captured by the Italians after being shot down over the Mediterranean and somehow managed to wangle her way into being sent home. If there was any way for her to make it off Malta, she would find it.

She took a deep breath, then smiled, feeling, if not happy, then hopeful for the first time in days. She patted Drake on the cheek. 'It's amazing what wisdom can come out of such a foolish person.'

The other pilots had been as surprised by Gwen's outburst as Drake and had stopped to watch anxiously, ready to step in if she lashed out at him, but now they laughed and Gwen felt a heavy weight lift from her as they welcomed her with open arms.

The available housing in the town which sprawled on the flatter land to the west of the mountain had been divided up quite sensibly. The Navy had naturally occupied the houses closest to the port and the RAC had taken those nearest the lifts to the base. The Army had had their choice of those that remained and had barracked their personnel close to where they were stationed on a daily basis, either close to the lifts for those men and women who manned the guns on the Rock, to the north for those that defended the isthmus, or to the south for those that serviced the guns pointing out to sea. The four storey house the Misfits had been assigned was, naturally, in the RAC section near the lifts, on the end of a terrace of houses occupied by the Spitsteam and Nelson aircrews. It had eight bedrooms of varying sizes, which, after the two couples had taken theirs, was enough for everyone who wanted one to have their own room, although Derek and Bruce elected to share one in order to keep each other company.

Gwen considered asking Scarlet to share a room with her as well, but didn't in the end, thinking that, knowing her, the Irishwoman would probably be coming and going at all hours, sneaking around the town and mountain. Instead, she lugged her newly-issued kitbag up to top of the house and found a moderately-sized room with a bed that would be big enough if Kitty did somehow manage to make her way to Gibraltar.

She opened the window and pushed the wooden shutters wide, letting fresh sea air in to clear out the musty smell that pervaded the house, which had probably been unoccupied since the owners had been evacuated at the beginning of the war.

There was a pleasant view out over the harbour and across the bay, but she barely saw it; instead her mind was flying eastward, towards the underground hospital on Malta, as she began imagining all the ways Kitty could make good her escape, as if picturing it could make it happen.

The pilots who had been on the Arturo were exhausted so, instead of looking around the rest of the town, the Misfits decided to rest for a couple of hours before wandering down the road for lunch.

The combined services mess Higgins had mentioned was maybe a quarter of a mile away, right on the harbour front. The building it was housed in had started life as a customs building and it was fairly draughty, but in the warm weather that wasn't such a bad thing. The large central room, where once upon a time cargoes were inspected, was filled with benches and long tables for informal dining, with all ranks eating shoulder to shoulder, while the smaller, but still sizeable rooms off to each side had been made into Officer's and NCO's messes, which were less frequented and only really used for formal occasions or if someone really wanted somewhere quiet for a drink or a meal.

With supplies plentiful there was quite a wide assortment of foodstuffs on the buffet table, with both Spanish and English cuisine represented and the Misfits took their time choosing before finding an empty table off to one side. They had thought to remain unobtrusive and keep to themselves, feeling the atmosphere and judging the mood of the men and women before entering into Gibraltar society, but they were recognised almost immediately and surrounded by people.

To begin with the questions came one at a time and were mostly about what had happened on Malta and how it had fallen and their answers were listened to in respectful hush, but then somebody asked about a family member who had been on the island, which opened the floodgates and names came shooting at them from all sides as if they'd come up through the clouds and found themselves in the middle of a pack of Fleas. Things became very loud and very chaotic as more and more men and women crowded around them, all wanting news of friends or loved ones and for a moment it looked like the Misfits were in real danger of being crushed, but then a deafening whistle, shrill as a banshee's shriek, reverberated around the room, making people cry out in pain. It was followed by a shout that was almost as loud as Scarlet jumped up onto the table.

'Oi! All of you! Shut up!' She glared down at the crowd, waiting for the last murmurs to die out before she continued at a more normal volume. 'We understand that you want to know about your friends and family, but we were stuck on an airbase most of the time we were on Malta. We didn't get out much and we certainly didn't meet *everyone* that was stationed there, so sorry, but we *can't* give you the answers you want. However, everyone who was evacuated from the island will be here soon and the admiral's office has already said that lists will be posted as soon as they're drawn up. You can see for yourselves then. Now, we were shipwrecked this morning. We're tired and hungry, could we just eat in peace please?'

She continued to glare until the people began to melt away, then stepped down and resumed eating as if nothing had happened.

The rest of the Misfits stared at her, their food momentarily forgotten.

'What?' she said around a mouthful of potatoes.

'Where on earth did you learn to whistle like that?' asked Wendy, her awe more than evident.

Scarlet shrugged as she swallowed. 'I used to herd sheep from Hummingbird, remember? How else do you think I could make myself heard?'

Half an hour later, after finishing off their meal with several mugs of tea and huge helpings of the various puddings on offer, the Misfits were just leaving the mess hall to head back to their house when a commotion drew them towards the harbour.

They stood silently at the edge of the water and watched as the launches came slowly in, each dragging at least half a dozen soot-blackened lifeboats, filled to the gunwales with exhausted survivors. They knew better than to ask if they could help with the unloading; the Navy had been taking care of such things for hundreds of years and they would just be getting in the way, so instead they went up and down the lines of men and women as they were deposited on the quay for assessing, doing what they could to comfort them and helping distribute food and water.

It took almost five hours to empty the lifeboats and get the Arturo's crew to either the hospital or accommodation in the town and, despite their own tiredness, the Misfits stayed the entire time. Only when the last was gone did they trudge up the slight rise to their house. Most of them went straight to bed after cleaning up, but the last thing Gwen heard before she slept was the creaking of a floorboard in the corridor as Scarlet, who'd taken the room next to her, tiptoed past on her way out.

Abby got up early the next morning and had left before any of the others were even awake. She came back just in time for breakfast with a wide smile on her face.

Owen would have raised an eyebrow at her if he'd had one, but after the bombing on the Arturo he couldn't even smirk properly anymore and had to be satisfied with loading his voice with as much sarcasm as possible, something that was easy to do with his lilting Welsh accent. 'You look like Scarlet did when she tried to sneak back in at two this morning.'

'You saw me?' said the Irishwoman, genuinely surprised.

Owen nodded. 'I was downstairs in the kitchen, getting myself a snack and you kept shushing yourself.'

'So that's why Higgins looks so bad this morning!' said Abby.

Scarlet grinned. 'Poor fellow can't hold his drink very well.'

Abby laughed. 'Compared to you, who can?'

Smiles faded slightly and there was a brief moment of silence as every one of the pilot answered Abby's question in their minds, even though it had been rhetorical - Mac had been the only one who had been able to keep up with Scarlet.

Abby took a deep breath to clear her head of the memory of the Scotsman crashing into the sea after saving the Arturo from a squadron of dive bombers before giving them the good news. 'So, I went to see Higgins and spoke to him about doing repairs and building a few new aircraft and he's happy with us to do that.'

'He doesn't know about the War Minister's orders, then?' asked Derek when the loud celebrations Abby's news had caused had died down.

'Oh, he knows about them alright,' said Abby with a grin. 'The message was relayed through here after all and the signalling station's on his base. He doesn't care, though, in fact his precise words were "hang the War Minister".'

It was almost twenty seconds until the cheering and laughter died down enough for her to continue. 'He has a few conditions, though.'

'I'm sure Scarlet will do anything he wants,' said Drake, with a wink.

'Hey! I'm the only one here who doesn't need any repairs or a new machine.' The Irishwoman glared at him for long seconds, but then turned to Abby, a broad smile on her face. 'Having said that...'

Abby rolled her eyes. 'Despite appearances, Higgins actually runs a fairly tight ship and it was a serious request on his part. He wants us to let a few people sit in on the design and construction of the new aircraft as classes for that unofficial university of his. And each of us will also be giving at least one lecture on the subject of his or her choice.'

Most of the pilots just nodded, accepting the condition - the majority of university degrees required senior students to tutor or lecture so they were used to it - but there were groans from Bruce, Wendy and Scarlet, who hadn't had any higher education and didn't particularly like speaking in public, at least not seriously.

Abby noticed their reluctance. 'You can make your talks more practical than theoretical if you want. Just don't blow anything up inside the mountain,' she looked pointedly at Wendy, then turned to Scarlet, 'or get anyone killed doing something silly like scaling the East Side or invading Africa.' Lastly she looked at Bruce. 'And as for you.'

The Australian grinned in anticipation, in a rare good mood that morning. 'Yes, Boss?'

'Drinking, carousing and Australian swearwords are not suitable topics.'

'Actually, I thought I'd talk about my experiences in the Indochine conflict, if that's alright with you, Boss.'

'Oh,' said Abby, pleasantly surprised. 'I'm sure that would be well received.'

'Yeah, there were some gorgeous Sheilas in Burma, I can tell you! And they did this thing with...'

Bruce was forced to duck as he was pelted by food from all sides and never got to finish his sentence.

'That's a lot of aircraft.'

'Yes, sir.'

'I mean, most of it is Italian rubbish, so no big loss, but still.'

Hans Gruber sipped at his coffee while he gazed idly through the Hal Far perimeter fence at the piles of scrap metal that had at one time been capable of soaring majestically through the air. They couldn't possibly represent more than a quarter of the aircraft the British had shot down, since most would have been lost in the sea, but there must have been at least a hundred in the field adjacent to what had been Misfit Squadron's base. Granted, many of them would have been brought down by anti-aircraft guns, but it still represented an impressive haul, even though the vast majority were Italian and therefore had been flown by inferior pilots.

Many of the aircraft looked like they had been cannibalised, which would go a long way towards explaining how the Misfits had been able to stay in the air so long when they hadn't been receiving supplies, but one machine stood out from all the rest - an enormous "Grand Eagle" bomber. It was on its own in a small clear area, closer up to the fence than any of the other aircraft, and had collapsed under its own weight, parts of it seemingly melted. What had happened to it was a mystery, but it was one he didn't particularly care to solve.

He stuffed the remains of a chocolate-covered pastry in his mouth, washed it down with the dregs of the coffee, then handed the cup off to Lang before wiping his hands on the cloth the steward offered.

'How long until you break through?' He turned from the aircraft graveyard and strode back towards the earthworks at the side of the airfield, near the ramp down to the underground airbase.

The army officer in charge of the excavation efforts was taken by surprise at the sudden switch in Gruber's focus and scrambled to catch up.

'Sometime today, sir. We have the concrete exposed and it's only a matter of...'

'I don't care about all that,' Gruber waved him into silence, 'just get me whatever's been left behind in that base.' The Misfits had been at Hal Far for months, they had settled in and made it their home. They must have left stuff behind in their hurry to depart and he wanted it, all of it, no matter what it was.

'Yes, sir, I...'

The poor man was cut off once again when a signals corporal ran up, a portable radio on his back. The man saluted the officers hastily before holding out the handset to Gruber.

'Sir, the admiral for you.'

Gruber grabbed the handset and pressed the button to transmit. 'Admiral, tell me you have good news at last.'

The admiral's voice, when it came after a couple of seconds, was distorted and the transmission rife with static, coming as it did from Sicily, but his words were clear nonetheless. 'We've received word from our spies in Algeciras that three Misfit aircraft were seen landing on Gibraltar yesterday morning, after the Arturo was sunk.'

Gruber didn't wait to hear anything more, he threw the headset in the general direction of the signalman and broke into a run for Hölle.

It was time to speak to the Kaiser.

CHAPTER 4

It had been an extremely busy couple of weeks.

The plans for the aircraft that had been built on Malta had gone down with the Arturo, along with just about all the other important papers from the island, so they needed to be redone. The design for Tanya's Wolf was easy enough to replicate, because it was identical to Lion and they had her as a reference. So was the one for Bruce's aircraft, Wraith, which had been based on Excalibur. Derek's aircraft had never been constructed, though, and, while he and Kitty had worked on it together, the American had done the majority of the work. After a few hours of scratching his head, trying to recall the details, he decided not to try to recreate it after all, but rather go back to his roots and design something that was all his own, like his first aircraft, Swift. He worked with Higgins' students and in four days managed to come up with *Kite*, which was loosely based on the birds of prey that could be seen over Gibraltar. She had a triangular tail and a wing shape like a recurve bow, with a slight upwards bend in the middle, similar to Excalibur's, but not quite as pronounced. When it was done he brought Abby and Gwen in to look it over and they quickly saw the potential of the aircraft, so Abby gave her approval for construction to go ahead, along with the others.

The lectures went just as well as the work on the aircraft did. They were supposed to take place in one of the small briefing rooms in the mountain base, like the ones given for the "university" courses, but when they proved to be a far bigger draw than anybody had expected, with more than five hundred people turned up for the first one, which was merely a discussion of military tactics by Derek, Higgins realised that he needed to find a bigger venue, especially seeing as bigger audiences were expected for the lectures imparted by Abby and Gwen. It made no sense for so many people to have to take the lifts up and down, either, so, instead of using the largest briefing room, it was decided to move the lectures to the Cathedral of St. Mary the Crowned in the town. The church had been abandoned since the Enlightenment, the religious relics long since sent to Rome, but the building itself had been maintained and it was easy enough for a crew of sailors to give the place a clean and a whitewash before setting up chairs and benches for more than a thousand "students". However, even then there had been people standing around the walls when Abby had given a tongue in cheek talk on "The History of Misfit Squadron" and when Gwen had lectured on Basic Aerodynamics the aisles had been filled with people sitting cross-legged on the flagstones.

Meanwhile, Bloodhound and Dreadnought were unpacked from their crates in the empty hangar and the pieces laid out so they could be checked over one by one, especially the delicate radar in Owen's machine. Bloodhound had barely been used in Malta, so she was quickly assembled and shifted to the side of the Misfits' hangar out of the way for servicing, but Dreadnought had suffered greatly in the final air battles and needed extensive repairs. Her crew, the "Whizz Bangers" had travelled to Gibraltar on Dreadnought, so they were on hand to work and they were joined by a gang of more than a hundred volunteers - the RAC fitters and mechanics who had nothing better to do and those mechanically minded men and women from the army and navy who leapt at the chance of doing something interesting with their off duty hours.

However, it was the repairs to the three surviving Misfit fighters which were given the highest priority. Some had been done on the Arturo, but it had been the bare minimum to keep them flying, as there just hadn't been any supplies to do them properly. Now, though, they were completely stripped down and the fitters went over them with a fine-tooth comb. Those bits which had been cobbled together from parts of enemy aircraft and didn't quite fit were discarded. The frames were checked over and any damaged pieces replaced. Most of the frayed cables were replaced as well, as was the wiring in the cockpits and quite a few instruments. Bald tyres were changed for new and, in some cases, so were entire braking mechanisms. The list of necessary work was endless, but eventually the pilots and fitters were satisfied with the innards of their machines and they turned their attention to the exteriors. Gwen had taken the opportunity to make small adjustments to the designs of the three aircraft and New Duralumin panels were shaped accordingly, then attached. Cracked, scratched and scavenged cockpit glass was changed for new. Several layers of paint were applied, then roundels, insignia and victory markings were put in place, before it was all brought to a high shine. Lastly, everything that needed lubricating was lubricated, fluid reservoirs were topped up, brand new springs were attached and then finally, after more than a week of work, all three aircraft were finished and the pilots were in their cockpits ready to fly.

It had been a busy week and extremely tiring, but it hadn't all been work. The pilots had had plenty of chance to rest, had eaten well, putting meat back onto their bones, and the little niggling injuries and maladies that they had picked up from not being able to take care of themselves properly had begun to clear up. Derek had even had a chance to sample the Spanish wines that somehow made their way into Gibraltar. Now, though, all they wanted was to be back in the air, not just to keep up their training, so that they would be ready to get back into the fight as soon as they got back to Britain, but because that was where they *belonged.*

Gwen moved her stick and rudders back and forth, feeling for obstructions or catches, while Giuseppe and her fitters, who had come through the shipwreck remarkably unscathed, went from one of her control surfaces to another to watch them and listen for squeaks or signs of misalignment. Everything was perfect, as expected, having been tested dozens of times before, but one more check was never too much.

The fitters finished their circuit of the aircraft and she received a thumbs up from Giuseppe just in time for Abby's voice to sound in her ears.

'Badger Leader to Badgers Two and Three. You ready?'

'Badger Two Roger, Leader.'

'Badger Three is good to go.'

'Right then, let's get up then shall we? Buttress this is Badger Leader, requesting permission to take off.'

'Buttress here, Badger Leader. Take off this morning is to the east. Taxi into position and hold for doors, please.'

'Roger, Buttress.' There was a click as Abby switched back to the squadron comms. 'Let's do this smartly, Badgers.'

Ordinarily Abby wouldn't worry about formations or tidiness when taking off; since everybody had different aircraft with different capabilities it was completely impractical. However, that afternoon they had a rather large audience, most of whom had worked on the aircraft, either directly or indirectly, and had come to witness the fruits of their labour. Giving them a good show was the least the Misfits could do to thank them for their help.

Gwen waited for Dragon to move forwards a few yards before releasing the brakes on Excalibur and the three aircraft rolled forward together in a V formation as did Drake the same on the other side of Abby. The only remotely tricky part was making the turn to line up with the hangar door, but Abby took it slow and wide, making it easy for her wingmates to stay with her, and brought them to a halt when they were perfectly lined up on the centre of the runway.

'Badger Flight ready for takeoff.'

'Roger, Badger Leader. Hangar door opening now.'

A thin crack appeared in the darkness directly in front of them, a brilliant line that was far brighter than the overhead lights in the hangar. It widened quickly, illuminating the end of the runway and making Gwen squint against the sudden glare. Thankfully, though, the sun wasn't shining directly into the hangar - it never really did apparently because of the runway's alignment - so even the tinted lens of her sub-standard standard-issue RAC lenses could deal with it.

In only a few short seconds the massive, enormously heavy door was open as wide as it went.

'Badger Flight, you are clear for takeoff.'

'Thank you, Buttress, see you soon.' Abby held her hand up and glanced to either side, making sure that Gwen and Drake were watching her, then twirled her finger. The pilots pushed their throttles forwards gently while keeping their brakes on, then, when the airscrews were buzzing like angry wasps and they were in danger of the new pads slipping, she dropped her hand sharply.

Brakes came off together and the three aircraft leapt forward in unison, accelerating strongly.

Standard procedure for fighters taking off from RAC Gibraltar was to get to takeoff speed just before reaching the end of the runway so as to minimise the risks of flying below a ceiling that was high as far as ceilings went, but close enough to punish a moment's inattention. Abby had decided that the Misfits would ignore procedure, though, and, as soon as all three aircraft had reached takeoff speed, they lifted a yard into the air and retracted their gear. They roared down the runway while maintaining that height, past the cheering men and women lined up in the Spitsteam hangar until they burst from the side of the mountain into the clean air. They soared into the sky, pulling up into a steep climb, and headed out over the Mediterranean.

Higgins had been very clear about where they could fly and where they couldn't. Obviously flying too south was out of the question with the Prussians controlling the airspace over and around Africa, but he had also told them that they were not permitted to fly north or east over Spanish territory.

Spain had been an ally of Britain since the War of Succession in the early seventeen hundreds, when Britain had helped the Austrian Habsburgs take power, and had only been belligerent to her during the period when Napoleon had ruled the country through his brother. After Napoleon was defeated and Spain returned to her people, they had rejected the return of the Habsburgs and declared themselves a Republic, following the example of the recently formed United States of America. Then, soon after Queen Victoria had brought Britain through the Enlightenment, they had done the same, rejecting the superstitions and oppression of the Catholic Church. For a while Spain had made huge advances in culture and learning, unseen since the days of the Caliphate of Córdoba. However, less than forty years later, the military, armed by Prussia and funded by radical parts of the church, had overthrown the Barcelona-based government and set themselves up in Madrid, the previous capital. So, despite Spain being ostensibly neutral and refusing to take part in the war, her military rulers owed their very existence to Prussia and were definitely far less lenient with British violations of their neutrality than they were with anyone else, going so far as firing on RAC aircraft or Royal Navy vessels that got just a little too close.

That was why Abby had decided to take them out over the water to test their machines. They would have plenty of room to play without having to worry about staying within certain boundaries. She didn't take them too far, though; Higgins had asked them to stay within easy sight of the Rock so that anyone who wanted to watch could do so.

'Right, then, Badgers, let's see what Gwen's improvements have done to our aircraft. Try to keep up.'

Without warning and almost before she had finished speaking, Abby threw her aircraft into a sharp corkscrewing dive.

Gwen all but leapt from her cockpit and jumped down from the wing. She hadn't realised how much a week without flying had affected her, making her feel even more grumpy and tired than Kitty's absence already had, but now she felt refreshed and full of energy.

She grinned at Giuseppe and her fitters who were waiting to take Excalibur in hand. 'She's wonderful, thank you! Don't change a thing!'

She nodded at them, then turned to go to the other pilots, but paused to take in the sight of Drake climbing carefully from his cockpit, moving like an old man. She chuckled and jogged over to him, arriving just in time to offer her hand to help him down from the wing.

Drake took it without thinking and slid heavily down to the ground.

'Getting old, Digger?'

'Oi! I'm only two years older than you!' He groaned and rubbed his lower back. 'No, it's this damn RAC flightsuit. It's no bloody use! And the week off didn't help either. I can't wait to get home and dig out my Gerber.'

'You've got a Gerber? Not a Petrov or a Johnson?' Gwen smiled. 'That's not very patriotic.'

'I bought it in Berlin in '37, before all this nonsense, and there's nothing unpatriotic about it if it's going to help me shoot down Prussians in comfort.'

Gwen grinned, ready to fire off another disparaging comment, but didn't when she noticed that Abby wasn't coming to debrief them as she usually did after a training flight. She looked over to Dragon and saw the group captain in conversation with Higgins, who was accompanied by a tall and roughly-dressed woman with a deep tan and shoulder-length black hair.

There were frowns on the faces of the two RAC officers and Gwen grimaced. 'Looks like bad news,' she said. 'Come on, let's see what's going on.'

They wandered over to them, Drake groaning and moaning at the effort of making his aching body move quick enough to keep up with them.

When they got to Dragon, Abby was shaking her head in disbelief at something. 'Won't the Spanish do anything to stop them?'

Higgins was about to answer her question, but stopped when Gwen and Drake approached. He smiled at them, but there wasn't much in the way of humour in it. 'Looks like you're going to have some fun while you're here after all.'

'Really?' asked Drake. 'More fun than giving lectures in a draughty old church? Impossible!'

Gwen nudged him in the ribs, drawing a groan. 'You do know that Bruce is back and you don't have to act the fool anymore, right?'

'Is he back?'

Gwen grimaced; he was right, Bruce might have recovered from his injuries, but, apart from all too brief moments of good humour, he wasn't back to his old self by any means.

Abby gave them a stern look and they lapsed into silence to allow Higgins to speak.

He gestured towards the dark-haired woman, who turned to look at them with intense dark eyes. 'This is Eulalia Balsells Carles. She was a pilot in the Iberian Civil War but now she works as our eyes and ears in north-eastern Spain. She's brought us some rather disturbing news, I'm afraid - Prussian armour has crossed the border between Spain and France and is on its way south.' He looked back to Abby. 'And, to answer your question, no, I doubt very much that the Spanish will do anything to stop them. They know they're only neutral for as long as the Kaiser says they are. If they move against them, or even just protest too strongly, that won't last a moment and they'll become a true puppet state. We may in fact find them adding to the forces arrayed against us, although by all accounts they wouldn't be able to bring very much to the table - their army is badly trained, what equipment they have is obsolete and their air force is almost non-existent. They only won their civil war because the Prussians and Italians essentially fought it for them.'

'Assuming the Spanish don't join in, what kind of forces are we talking about?'

'Two heavy divisions, so at least six hundred armoured vehicles of various types.'

Drake whistled. 'That's a lot of tanks. Are we sure they're coming here, though?'

Higgins looked to the woman and she nodded and answered in American-accented English. 'Yes. My people were able to speak with some Prussian officers and it is common knowledge among them that they are coming here. They should arrive in a week or two.'

'But why?' asked Abby. 'Taking this place will cost them dearly and they've never seemed bothered before.'

'Maybe there's something here right now that they want.' Higgins said, looking pointedly at the three pilots.

Abby scoffed. 'Surely not us!'

'It's Gruber.' Drake said, suddenly certain. 'This has to be his doing.'

'Gruber?' The Spanish woman asked, mangling the word horribly, her tongue not quite wrapping itself around it. She looked at Higgins.

'That is the name I was trying to tell you. *That* is who they blame for having to leave their comfortable quarters in France.'

The Misfit pilots shared a look.

Drake laughed. 'Persistent little blighter, isn't he? I'm beginning to think he's got something against you Misfits personally.'

'*Us* Misfits, Digger,' said Abby. 'You're one of us now.'

'Damn,' said Drake. He sighed, then suddenly turned to Higgins, drew himself up and saluted smartly. 'Requesting a transfer, sir!'

Higgins stared at him in bemusement for a moment, then shook his head and looked at Abby. 'I take it you're not too concerned about this threat then?'

'Not really. You did say this place was "unassailable" after all.'

Higgins smiled weakly. 'Yes. I did say that, didn't I?'

After Higgins reassured them that he would let them know everything that Eulalia had to report, the Misfits made their way to the ready room at the back of the hangar to freshen up. Justine Charmers had been lurking nearby, just out of earshot, waiting to speak to them. She intercepted them half-way there and fell into step beside Abby.

'I was watching your flight,' she smiled, 'actually, most of my squadron was.'

Abby smiled sideways at her. 'I hope we didn't disappoint.'

'On the contrary, it was extremely impressive and eye-opening. Especially the way you pass from one manoeuvre to the next. It's seamless, there's no pause for thought, you all just seem to know instinctively what to do. Can you teach us that? Or is it because of your machines?'

Abby shook her head. 'Our aircraft have nothing to do with it - there are some incredible pilots out there flying Spitsteams and Harridans - you just have to know your own intimately. *But* you also need talent and a heck of a lot of experience and that *isn't* something that can be taught.' She chuckled gently at Charmers' disappointed pout. 'That doesn't mean there's nothing that my pilots can't teach yours, though. Why don't we fly with you next time you go up and we'll see what we can do?'

Charmers' face lit up. 'That would be most appreciated, thank you, ma'am!'

They were at the door to the ready room now and Abby stopped, letting Gwen and Drake go in, before turning to face the squadron leader. 'You're due up in, what?' She consulted her chronograph. 'An hour?'

'Yes, ma'am.'

'Right, then. I'm going to have a cup of tea, but as soon as I'm done I'll come and find you and we'll discuss what you want to do.'

'Thank you!' Charmers smiled widely, then hurried away, a new bounce in her step.

Abby watched her go for a few seconds, then followed her pilots into the ready room. They were at the side of the room, filling plates with food to go with their tea, but they were surrounded by the rest of the Misfits, who all looked up as she came in.

'How reliable is this woman's report?' asked Wendy, her voice full of scepticism. 'Even the Prussians aren't crazy enough to attack Gibraltar.'

'I agree!' Derek called out. 'It's so tactically unsound as to be absurd! With the fall of Malta, Crete and Greece, Gibraltar isn't nearly as important as it was before. They already have naval bases nearby so they have nothing really to gain. And even with, what was it, two armoured divisions? They'll still be hard-pressed to take the Rock. To be sure of a good result they'll need support from the air force and navy and a lot of it, but they'll still lose...' his forehead wrinkled in thought, 'at least three-quarters of their forces, I reckon, if not more. And who knows where they'll get all that from and what they'll leave vulnerable when they lose most of it. It's just not worth it! I just can't believe that any of their commanders would be so daft as to even try!'

Drake smirked at Abby. 'Shall I tell them who ordered the attack?'

'Be my guest. You seem to have let slip everything else, you might as well make it a grand slam.'

He grinned and gave her a small bow, then began to speak, widening his eyes dramatically, and declaiming in an ominous tone like a bad Shakespearean actor. 'The name of the person who has put these portentous events in motion is known the world over. It belongs to a man who is praised and worshipped by some, but hated and reviled by others.' He hunched over slightly as he looked around the group and lowered his voice to almost a whisper, as if speaking in confidence to them. 'It is a name which has become an obscenity on the lips of the soldiers marching south to their deaths, though. They whisper it in messes, they curse it in bars and they call it out during their nightmares. And that name...'

'Oh, do get on with it,' interrupted Gwen with a grin, deliberately putting him off his stride at the very climax of his speech.

'*That name...*' Drake said again, raising his voice and shooting a petulant look at Gwen, 'is...'

'It's Gruber, isn't it?' said Derek with a sigh.

'*Gruber!*' Drake announced enigmatically, spreading his hands wide in triumph. Nobody was listening to him, though; they were all staring at Derek.

'Gruber's behind this?' asked Owen incredulously with only a quick, amused glance at Drake. His astonishment disappeared almost instantly, though, and he shrugged. 'Actually, that would explain it; the Kaiser would do anything for his golden boy.'

'Even so,' said Derek. 'This isn't a few extra ships and aircraft to overwhelm Malta, this is an entire army to try to conquer something that is better defended than the British Isles and worth an awful lot less! The Kaiser must be out of his mind.'

'There was the suggestion that there was added incentive to try to take Gibraltar now.'

'What? *Us?*' Scarlet said with a laugh, instantly catching on to what Abby was implying. 'I hope we're still valued as highly as this after the war; think of the jobs we could land! No, forget that! Think of the *husbands!*'

When the laughter died down, Abby spoke to them seriously. 'Up to now we've been taking our time with repairs and construction, but now I want all hands on deck. I want the new aircraft finished by the end of the week and Dreadnought back in action. Wendy, we're also going to need something to punch through the Prussian armour and there's a lot of it, so a few rockets aren't going to be enough. Any ideas you have would be appreciated.'

Wendy rubbed her hands together eagerly. 'My pleasure.'

'Owen, poke around the radar installation, please. Make sure everything's working as well as it could.'

'Roger.'

'And Derek, see if you can find who's in charge of the tactical plan for defence, please. *If* there is one. It's probably some army type, so have patience and don't use too many long words when you poke holes in it.'

That brought more laughter from most of the pilots, but Derek frowned. 'I'm only an amateur tactician, Abby, I don't think it's my place to advise the professionals.'

'I know, but I'm thinking that, even if they dismiss your advice out of hand, they might start to do a bit of thinking for themselves and improve something that's probably been in place since the First Great War, instead of just sitting back and waiting for the Prussians to come.'

'Alright then.'

'Thank you.' She gave him a reassuring smile then addressed the pilots at large. 'We're also going to start training with the Spitsteam squadrons. Charmers already requested that we give her people a few pointers and that was before we knew what was coming. Gwen, Drake and I are going to go up for at least two training flights a day, but as soon as the other aircraft are ready I want everyone taking part.'

'The Spit pilots are green as grass,' said Bruce, 'it's going to take more than a week or two to knock them into any kind of shape.'

Abby gave him a hard look. 'I know that, but we're going to do our best anyway.'

'Of course, Boss.' The Australian grinned. 'Just as well we didn't really want that month off.'

'Don't complain. You know you would have just got bored.'

'Nah, Boss, I wouldn't. I'm having far too much fun giving lectures to *ever* get bored.'

'I'll let Higgins know you've volunteered to give more, then, shall I?' Abby said, smiling sweetly.

Bruce sighed exaggeratedly and shook his head. 'I'm *really* sorry. I wish I could, but I don't think I'm going to have time, what with all the building and flying and such.'

'We'll see...' Abby gave him a wolfish look, which had him swallowing nervously, then turned to look at the other pilots. 'Whatever reason the Prussians have for coming, they *are* coming and I have a feeling this fight is going to make Malta look like bonfire night, so we need to make sure everything is as ready as it can be. So, if you can think of anything that will make our chances of survival better, then speak up, no matter how outlandish your idea - it's not as if they don't have the materials to build whatever we come up with.'

The pilots nodded, but Wendy grinned and rubbed her hands together in glee as something occurred to her. 'We're going to get to see the big guns in action!'

'Yes,' said Drake dryly. 'And that will make it all worthwhile.'

CHAPTER 5

While those Misfits who were still constructing their aircraft redoubled their efforts, Abby, Gwen and Drake took the two Spitsteam squadrons in hand. They divided the pilots into two groups. Those who had been sent to Gibraltar fresh out of flight school and only had the experience of the daily patrols - some ten men and women, mostly in their early twenties - were assigned to Drake, who, as a former RAC instructor, would be able to assess their basic manoeuvres and smooth out any rough edges. The rest, the ones who were secure in the handling of their aircraft and had managed to get some combat experience before shipping out, either in France or, in a couple of cases, over Britain, were shared between Gwen and Abby, who would try to get them ready to face the vastly experienced Fliegertruppe pilots.

Higgins showed up just as the Misfits and their charges were performing final checks for their first flight. The Spanish woman, Eulalia, was with him, dressed in a black leather flightsuit with four inch-thick parallel red lines running diagonally across it from her left shoulder to her right hip.

'Group Captain!'

Abby stopped what she was doing as he called out to her. 'Sir?' She came out from under Dragon's wing, where she'd been inspecting the ailerons.

'Would you mind if Eulalia here joined you? She has asked to take part in the defence and would like to get her eye back in after spending the last few months grubbing around in the dirt for us.'

Abby smiled at the young woman. 'I don't mind one bit. Do you have a Spitsteam for her?'

The woman shook her head and answered for herself. 'No need. I have my own aircraft.' She smiled over her shoulder. 'Ah, here she comes now.'

Abby glanced in the direction the woman was looking, expecting one of the stubby Polikasparovs that the Republicans had used in the civil war, but her jaw dropped at the sight of the machine that RAC fitters, on an RAC base, were pushing into place next to a long line of RAC Spitsteams - a Muhlenberg MU9.

It was just about the most incongruous thing she'd ever seen, but at least it wasn't painted in Prussian colours - it was a shiny black, with two red stripes on each wing to match the ones on the woman's flightsuit.

Abby turned back to Eulalia and found her smiling knowingly. 'Would you like a closer look?'

Abby found herself nodding mutely and coughed, trying to regain her composure. 'Yes. Yes I would. I'll finish my checks and meet you over there.'

'Very well, Group Captain.' The woman nodded to her, then turned to Higgins. 'Thank you, Bob, fins després.'

'Have a good flight, Eulalia!' Higgins grinned at her. He threw a casual salute at Abby, then sauntered off down the line of Spitsteams and began exchanging pleasantries with his pilots, trying to calm their obvious nerves at the prospect of flying with the vaunted Misfit Squadron.

Abby finished her checks in record time and left Dragon in the care of Sergeant Potter, her chief fitter, while she made her way over to the black aircraft. Before she had taken more than half a dozen steps she was joined by Gwen and Drake, who were just as interested as she was in getting a closer look at the machine.

'Well, it's an A or B, isn't it? Just look at that nose.'

Drake's observation had Gwen and Abby nodding - there were two machine guns mounted in the distinctive squarish nose, which only the early variants had had. They had been their only weapons, making them not only under-armed, but less streamlined than the later versions, which did away with them.

'The wings aren't original, though,' said Abby. 'And it looks like she's got two cannon and two more machine guns in them.'

Gwen grunted and shook her head. 'You two have been spending too much time with Wendy. The only reason to care about how many guns an aircraft has is to calculate the effect of the weight. I'm more interested in seeing what else she's done to it.'

The Spanish woman was speaking to one of the RAC fitters who'd brought the aircraft out, but she broke off as the Misfits approached and smiled in welcome.

'So. What do you think of my aircraft? My *Llibertat*?'

Gwen smiled at the name of the MU9; "Freedom" in the Catalan language seemed entirely appropriate for a machine "liberated" from the Prussians and used to fight for that freedom. 'She's beautiful.'

Abby nodded in agreement. 'She is. Very. More so because of the modifications you've made to make her your own and a little less... Prussian.'

'Yes. Exactly!' Eulalia said enthusiastically. 'A friend of mine was a talented designer and she helped me to make her truly special.'

A note of sadness had entered her voice when she'd mentioned her friend, but it was gone as quickly as it had appeared and she smiled again as she gestured towards the aircraft. 'Come with me while I do my checks? She has been well cared for, but after four months in storage you can understand I want to see for myself that she is OK.'

Eulalia explained that the two cannons were recent additions, presents from Higgins, as was the new hydromatic airscrew and an Ozymandias spring, but the rest of the modifications had been made during the civil war. The most striking changes were the wings, which were now elegantly curved, quite different from the straight-edged, very functional, very Prussian wings it had once had, and the canopy - the distinctive cuboid canopy of the MU9 was gone, replaced by something akin to the bubble-shaped canopy of a Spitsteam. There were dozens of other changes, though, of varying sizes and importance, all adding up to a machine, which, in Gwen's assessment at least, was going to be deadly and effective in the air, despite it having started life as an aircraft that was now at least three years out of date - it was indeed an MU9A, one of the first models ever produced.

By the time Eulalia had finished her inspection, and the Misfits had returned to their aircraft, the Spitsteam pilots had done theirs as well and were in their cockpits waiting for Abby to give the signal to take off.

'All right then, Badgers, let's see what we have to work with,' Abby said over the Misfits' radio frequency before switching to the general one. 'Buttress, this is Badger Leader. Duckling Squadron is ready to fly.'

As Bruce had so aptly put it, the pilots, at least the younger ones, *were* green as grass and even the more experienced ones had grown rather rusty with so little to do apart from go on patrols. That didn't mean they were lost causes, though, after all, they had far more hours of flight time under their wings than many of the men and women who had been thrust into the air over the previous summer over Britain.

It was generally accepted that there were three types of pilots. There were those who flew by the numbers, so to speak, performing manoeuvres as the textbook laid them down. Then there were those who flew by instinct, who did things with their aircraft more because it felt right, rather than because they'd been told it was possible and whose basic technique was usually quite sloppy. There was a decent mix of those types in the two squadrons based in Gibraltar, but, thankfully, none of the pilots were the third kind, the ones who had no feel for their aircraft or enough training to be able to handle it in more than the most basic of ways - with the desperate days of the previous summer gone, there was no longer any need to throw unprepared men and women into the air.

The Misfits didn't agree with that assessment and maintained that there was a fourth type of pilot, one that combined the best of the first two in someone who was capable of carrying out perfect manoeuvres while retaining the flexibility and instincts to break the rules when it was called for. Someone whose relationship with their aircraft was almost symbiotic, giving them an understanding that allowed them to push their aircraft to the very edge and not just to what was seen as their limits. Someone who could assess the situation around them in all three dimensions, almost sensing it, rather than seeing it, and instantly know how to act accordingly. *That* was the kind of pilots *they* were and that was what they would have liked to make of the Spitsteam pilots. Unfortunately, it was impossible for the vast majority of pilots to attain such a high level of mastery, which was one reason why there weren't more elite squadrons like the Misfits, but, to their surprise, they found two pilots who might be able to.

One was a pilot in Drake's group - Aviator Sergeant Ian Taylor. He was only nineteen, but he already had plenty of flight experience because his family ran a company on the Isle of Wight that provided flying tours of the island and he had begun acting as copilot for his mother and father at twelve. It took Drake less than twenty minutes to realise the boy's potential and he immediately sent him to join Abby's group for more advanced training.

The other was Eulalia. The woman's aircraft was just as impressive as Gwen had known it would be, incredibly manoeuvrable and, with the new airscrew and spring, just as fast as Dragon and Lion. However, it was her skill in handling Llibertat that made all the difference and, when the exercises were over and it came to the mock dogfights, she defeated all of the Spitsteam pilots easily. She had no chance against the Misfits, though, but that was more because she was out of practice than because she was any less skilled than them.

They flew three sorties that day and saw a marked improvement in every single one of the pilots, as if they had just needed a bit of a kick up the arse to get them into gear. The biggest changes took place in the two that they had singled out, though. As Eulalia got her hand back in the rough edges smoothed out of her flying and she showed herself to be at least as competent as Gwen, if not as brilliant as Abby, and the young RAC pilot, Ian Taylor, made a giant leap forwards as if the cogs had just clicked into place within him.

The three pilots were understandably very pleased, therefore, with how the first day of flying had gone, but the other Misfits also had reason to be happy and it was a far more optimistic squadron that met in the sparsely furnished sitting room of the house to give an update on their progress over a nightcap before bed.

Repairs on Dreadnought and the construction of the new aircraft were proceeding apace and were dealt with quickly, then it was time for the others to make their reports.

'The defence plans are outdated, to say the least.' Derek said as he topped up his white wine. 'They were drawn up in 1912, at a time when there weren't any guns on the mountain, and haven't been looked at since. In fact, none of the officers at army headquarters even knew where the diagrams and documents were when I asked to see them! They finally found them in a box in the basement, which had been used as a nest for a family of mice and, as you can probably imagine, they weren't in very good condition. I managed to clean off enough droppings and mildew to make them out, but I shouldn't have bothered; they're based around the premise that an attack will consist of an infantry charge across the isthmus and rely on the wall to stop it.' He grimaced and took a sip of his wine, as if to rid himself of a bad taste. 'I've seen the wall. One of the first things I did when we got here was to walk it. Admittedly, it must have been quite strong in its day and would have done a good job, but it's almost a hundred and fifty years old now and has big chunks missing because, over the last couple of decades, much of the stone has been sneaked away by the locals and used to build houses. An effort was made to make an approach across the isthmus difficult during the first war, but we're only talking about a few dozen strings of barbed wire, which have been rusting there ever since. They wouldn't stop a drunk Spaniard, let alone a tank! And they haven't even bothered to mine it because a few of the more horticultural-minded officers have allotments outside the wall and they don't want them to blow themselves up! There is *nothing* that would stop even the *smallest* of Prussian tanks from barging straight across and into the town.' He chuckled wryly. 'My favourite part of the plan was the provision for a cavalry charge coming from the northern gate to flank any invaders who make it to the wall. The staff officers had left an aide to deal with me, a young captain who had obviously been told to get rid of me as quickly as possible, and when I called his attention to *that* he started trying to defend it, saying that the cavalry would be able to ride out with some of those new magnetic grenades the army likes so much. He got quite enthusiastic, in fact, and began expounding on the idea. Until I pointed out that there *aren't* any horses in Gibraltar.'

Derek was becoming more and more indignant and worked up as he went on and when he paused for another sip of his wine Abby quickly interjected. 'And are they going to do anything to update the defences?'

'No, they're not. In the end, the aide waved off my concerns and said that they weren't going to reinforce the defences because they just needed to "fire the guns at the enemy".'

'That sounds pretty good to me!' said Wendy with a grin.

'With the amount of artillery they have on the mountain I thought so too. But then I found out that they only have two hundred shells for those two monstrosities on the summit.'

'Two hundred shells each?' asked Abby.

Derek shook his head. 'Between them. I also found out that the shells are more like glorified cannon balls than anything else; they rely entirely on their weight rather than explosives for their destructive force. Which is perfect for large targets like ships, but you'd need a direct hit to take out a tank.'

'So, even if they save them for the Walkers or those heavy tanks, the Goths...'

'*Goethes*,' chimed in Wendy, grinning happily. 'Bloody huge blighters they are! I'm *really* looking forward to seeing *them* up close!'

'Yes, thank you, Wendy.' Abby chuckled. 'So. *If* they save the shells for the Walkers and the *Goethes*, which the smaller artillery can't put a dent in, then they're only going to have two hundred shots to kill the dozen or so they're bringing. Sounds like the gunners are going to have to make good practice.'

'That's the thing,' said Derek, 'they've *never* practised. The guns haven't been fired since they were first tested.'

'What? Not even at enemy ships going past?' asked Wendy. 'I can't believe that gunners, of all people, wouldn't want to take a few potshots at least.'

'I was told that what few enemy ships enter the Mediterranean sneak past at night and that army policy is not to waste shells trying to hit them. They're not particularly accurate against moving targets at more than ten miles anyway, apparently.'

Abby grimaced. 'So, you're saying we can't rely on Victoria and Victor.'

'I'm not saying that, exactly, just that we shouldn't pin too many of our hopes on them.'

'There's a whole lot of other guns on the mountain, Abby,' Wendy said.

Abby nodded. 'Yes, but they have a much shorter range than the "Vees" and I was hoping that we'd be able to halt the Prussians before they got that close. At the moment that doesn't look too likely, though, so we need a backup plan.' She turned back to Derek. 'I'll speak to Higgins tomorrow and see if he can't get whoever is in charge to listen to any ideas you come up with.'

'Thank you!' Derek smiled and rubbed his hands eagerly. 'I have quite a few already. In fact, I've been discussing this very subject with some like-minded men and women in the evenings and we've speculated that a Roman...'

Abby held up a hand to stop him before he launched into one of his lectures on the tactics of the ancient world. 'No need to elaborate; I'm sure you'll do a wonderful job. Having said that, I'd rather not *have* to rely on static defences, no matter how good.' She turned to Wendy. 'Have you come up with anything that will help us to, ahem, stop those tanks in their tracks?'

Most of the pilots groaned at Abby's choice of phrase, but the big woman didn't seem to notice, she just smiled broadly, her thoughts having already turned to her favourite pastime.

'Higgins' students have definitely come up with a few interesting ways to blow things up, but unfortunately there's nothing we can put on our aircraft. I have had a few thoughts of my own, though, but I want to think them through a bit better before I present them.'

'Alright,' Abby nodded, then looked to Owen. 'Next. Please tell me that those antennae...' she frowned and broke off mid-sentence. 'Antennae? Antennas? Which is it?'

'Antennas,' said Derek. 'It's antennae for insects and such, antennas for all that,' he waved his hand dismissively, '*stuff* that Owen does.'

Owen's mouth twisted into a lopsided grin. 'That "stuff" was instrumental in keeping Britain safe last summer and it's going to keep us safe now. Much more than any of your birds and bees will.'

Derek scoffed. 'My studies of the creatures of the air have produced several aircraft, which...'

'Ahem!' Abby cut him off and gave the two men a scathing look, which rendered them silent before they could launch into a good-natured argument that the Misfits had heard dozens of times. 'I've warned you two about bickering like old women around me. If you keep it up I will tie you to weather balloons and make you act as spotters for the guns.'

'Sorry, Abby.'

'Sorry, Abby.'

Both men looked so much like scolded children that the rest of the pilots couldn't help but laugh.

Abby joined in, but turned serious and got back on target as soon as the noise had died down.

'As I was saying - I take it the *antennas* on the mountain actually do something, Owen.'

The Welshman nodded. 'The antennas are fine, but the radar itself is old, inaccurate and fairly short ranged. It's actually one of the ones we got rid of in England a couple of years ago, when I was helping overhaul the system.'

'Waste not want not,' said Drake, upending a wine bottle over his glass to drain the dregs.

'Indeed,' said Owen.

'Will it warn us if the Prussians try anything?' asked Abby, concerned.

Owen nodded. 'It'll do what it needs to, but I'll give it a few tweaks anyway; this model is prone to giving false readings. They've been able to live with that until now, confirming their readings visually or sending up a Spit to investigate, but that's not ideal and not something we want right now.'

'Alright, thank you.' Abby drained her glass and looked around. 'Well, it's late and we've got a lot of flying to do tomorrow. Has anyone else got anything they want to say?'

'Actually, yes,' Owen said. 'I know I'm stating the obvious here, but we need replacements. Are those two pilots good enough to join you fighter drivers?'

Abby looked at Gwen. 'What do you think?'

'I...' Gwen began but had to stop when a lump welled up in her throat. Now she knew how Abby had felt when she had joined the squadron as a replacement for her fallen sister, Cece. Finding replacements made the losses seem more real, somehow. It was like finally admitting that they were never coming back. It was just as well she didn't have to do that for Kitty yet; she didn't think she'd be able to take it.

She took a deep breath and forced herself to think back to the day's flying, concentrating on analysing the pilots' abilities and trying to ignore what she was being asked to analyse them for.

'Uh, Eulalia is certainly good enough. She has good instincts, her technique is almost flawless and she handles that Nine better than any Prussian. Sergeant Taylor is pretty raw right now, though. He has a lot of potential, but that's all it is right now. Although, if he continues to improve as much as he did today, he may well realise that potential by the time the convoy gets here to take us home.'

'My thoughts almost exactly,' said Abby. 'I think they would make excellent additions to the squadron. Unfortunately, though, their ability isn't the only thing we have to take into consideration, there's their availability as well. Taylor, for example, is a serving pilot assigned to a remote station without a ready replacement and we may be told we can't have him until there is one available.'

Owen shrugged. 'If the War Ministry has any sense there will be a few squadrons of pilots and aircraft coming with the convoy, so hopefully that won't be a problem.'

Abby chuckled. 'Since when has the Ministry had any sense? Or the Minister? And as for Eulalia - we know nothing about her beyond what little Higgins has told us. She could be working for the Prussians for all we know and there's also the fact that she's Spanish and the way things are going they might be at war with us soon.'

She smiled apologetically at Gwen before continuing. 'I wish Kitty were here; she might have run into her while she was here, or at least heard of her.' She looked around at the pilots. 'Let's keep an eye on them for now and if we still want either of them by the time the convoy gets here I'll approach Higgins.' She yawned. 'Now, it's way past my bed time, so if anybody else wanted to say something it can wait until tomorrow. Good night all.'

Choruses of good nights followed her out of the door, as did most of the pilots, but Gwen stayed, struggling to deal with the emotions that Abby's words had brought surging up from where she'd so recently buried them. On the Arturo she'd dealt with her frustrations and fears by drinking and she was sorely tempted to grab a couple of the bottles from the sideboard, take them up to her room and forget her troubles that way for a few hours. That was only a temporary measure, though, and ultimately would solve nothing. It certainly wouldn't bring Kitty any closer to home. Besides, flying cleared her head much better, without leaving such a bad feeling afterwards, and if she turned up in the morning smelling of alcohol Abby might take that away from her. There was no way she was going to risk that happening; flying was the one good thing left in her life at that moment. So, she remained where she was, listening to friends, who had tried their best but couldn't do anything to help her, make their way to their bedrooms, wishing there was someone waiting for her in hers, and staring into her empty glass.

Bruce nursed his drink, waiting for everyone to go upstairs to bed, as he had the past few nights. However, that night Gwen showed no sign of going. She didn't seem to be paying attention to anything around her, though, she was just sitting there with a distant look on her face. She was more than likely thinking about Kitty, which meant she would be completely dead to the world around her for a good quarter of an hour or more, so he just waited patiently until the creaking of floorboards and closing of doors on the floors above died down, then stood and made his way quietly from the house, leaving her where she was.

Wherever armed forces were stationed, whether in peacetime or war, there was always something to entertain them, to stop men and women who could die at any moment and wanted to spend their time as enjoyably as possible from getting bored or frustrated and taking it out on the real estate, or each other. There were the officially sanctioned establishments, like the messes, stocked with plentiful food and drink, and the dance halls, where more energetic desires could be satisfied, but most places also had a good selection of illicit activities, run behind the scenes, very much in the shadows.

With secure supply lies, and plenty of more than willing locals, the leisure facilities he'd enjoyed in Burma had been top notch, whereas in Malta they had understandably been extremely thin on the ground. The situation in Gibraltar wasn't nearly as bad as it had been on Malta, but, with no willing locals, some of the more carnal entertainments were sorely lacking. However, that didn't mean there wasn't a wide range of things to appeal to even the most jaded Australian: there were illicit stills providing extremely strong liquor far cheaper than the messes; a club where men and women could fight for money (or just because they enjoyed it); there were even a couple of places where more intoxicating substances could be consumed, although that was a little deeper than even Bruce liked to sink. His destination that night wasn't any of those places, though, he was only interested in one thing and that was *cards*.

He'd first gotten a taste for poker back home in Australia, it being the game of choice when it was raining and a game of cricket was out of the question, at least for those who didn't like more "intellectual" games like chess or bridge. However, when he'd come to England and joined the squadron he'd found that, of the pilots, only Kitty shared his passion. It was only natural, then, that the two of them had started playing together.

Up till that point, he'd thought he was rather good; he'd been by far the best player in his squadron and, with all the poker they'd played during the rains of the monsoon season, he would have been rich by the end of the Indochine skirmishes if they'd been playing for money, but she was so much better than him and quickly put paid to that idea - she'd been playing poker since she could count, as something to do on the frequent train rides from the Wright family's estates in Ohio to New York City, where they did their business and where she had gone to school. She had taken him under her wing, teaching him tricks and intricacies of the game that he hadn't even been aware of and they had practised those new skills wherever the squadron had been based. However, unlike those games, which had been played among friends for matchsticks or whatever else there was to hand, the stakes in the gambling den in the deserted back street of Gibraltar were *very* real.

Having not received any pay in months, he hadn't had any cash to use as a stake at first, but the thoroughly unscrupulous sailor who ran the joint, who everyone knew as "Jack Tar", was more than willing to give his customers credit, at extortionately high interest, advising them that he had "relations" in London who would collect if they were posted home and tried to renege on their debts. The standard of the other players was generally quite low, though, and he won far more than he lost. He was able to pay the man back in one night's play and went on to accrue a tidy sum in the following couple of nights, but he wasn't really playing for the money, nor was he even trying too hard to win. No, he was there because playing poker made things seem normal, like nothing had changed.

Like his friends were still alive.

He'd thought he was lucky. After all, he had commanded a squadron during the Indochine skirmishes, one of the bloodiest conflicts in recent history, and managed to bring most of his boys home alive.

Everything had gone to hell since he had joined the Misfits, though.

France had been fun for a while, but quickly turned into a complete fiasco and they'd lost Cece. Then, a few months later in Muscovy the girl he hooked up with turned out to be a Prussian spy and had killed Mac's girlfriend, sending the Scotsman into a spiral for which he was to blame. But everything had come to a head in Malta when pilots had started dropping like flies. Mac, Chastity, Chalky, poor Monty. The best of them, all dead, along with the poor Navy pilots who'd joined them. And in the end it had all been for nothing; they hadn't even been able to hold on to the islands.

The Misfits were jinxed and things weren't going to get any better while the War Minister had them in his sights, in fact they would probably get worse, if that was possible. More than once, since leaving Malta, he had considered requesting a transfer and getting out before he had to watch any more of his friends die. Not that there were that many left.

While he'd been lost in thought, his feet had carried him to the gambling den without him realising and he went down the tight alleyway next to it and into the tiny back garden. A coded knock on the back door was answered by a click as the bolt was slid back and he slipped through the gap, past the blackout curtain hung in the opening, and into a small kitchen.

'Evening, Bruce.'

'Jemmy.' Bruce gave the brutish sailor who guarded the door a nod without slowing his step and went straight through into the gaming rooms.

Originally the house had had separate dining and sitting rooms on the ground floor, but the wall between them had been taken down to create a single moderately-sized space for the gambling tables. Word had quickly spread about the new "casino", as Jack Tar rather optimistically dubbed it, and more and more entertainment-starved people had begun to turn up until it was packed to overflowing and some of them had to be turned away. However, before those spurned people could become annoyed and perhaps snitch to the authorities,

Jack had simply had his men knock through into the empty house next door and opened a second gaming room there to accommodate them.

The original gaming room, just past the kitchen, was given over to the louder, more raucous games, like dice and roulette, for those who just wanted to blow off some steam. It was crowded that night, as it was twenty-four hours a day (the casino never closed) and the bar along one wall was doing a roaring trade, but these weren't really gamblers, they had just come to have some fun. The serious gambling went on in the second room in the adjoining house, through a heavy blackout curtain that blocked most of the noise, and that was where Bruce headed.

There were only a couple of dozen people on this side of the establishment, sitting at the four large card tables spaced evenly around the room - two for blackjack, one for baccarat, one for poker. There was no bar in here to encourage casual visitors to stay either, just a couple of waitresses in tight black cocktail dresses, off-duty sailors, constantly moving around and quietly taking orders.

It was quiet and cosy, the lighting dimmed and the furniture expensive and comfortable, which conspired to create an atmosphere of class, like some old-style gentlemen's club, and was designed to coax the gamblers into staying longer than they should and losing more than they would. That image was only slightly ruined by the presence of the two burly sailors on either side of the entrance, keeping beady eyes on the gamblers, and the throne-like chair in a shadowy corner, which was where Jack Tar sat on those occasions when he visited.

Bruce didn't notice the men who glared at him as he pushed through the curtain, nor did he glance in the direction of the throne to see if there was an audience to the games; his eyes were fixed on the table in the far corner, the one dedicated to poker.

He made his way directly to it, pausing only to ask a waitress to bring him a scotch, and sat in one of the empty chairs.

He played as he always did: casually, putting the minimum of effort into the management of his cards and barely taking any notice of his fellow players, mostly regulars, beyond the tells he'd previously and extremely easily identified. Having never spoken to them, beyond asking for cards, he didn't even know their names, to him they were just Captain Twitch, Sergeant Ear Tug, Private Scratch, Corporal Smirk, Lieutenant Lip Bite and such.

He had finished his first scotch and was well into his second before he noticed that the stack of coins on the table in front of him was dwindling rather than growing as it usually did. He peered around the table, looking past the cards to the piles in front of the other players. Most were rather smaller than they had been, which was to be expected after more than an hour's play with him, but one had swollen to prodigious size, which was usually the prerogative of his own.

He lifted his eyes further and for the first time properly took in the woman sitting almost directly across from him. She was an army officer, a captain, with brown hair that fell just below her shoulders and caramel coloured eyes. She wasn't beautiful, having a nose that was a shade too large and a rather masculine jawline, but there was a glint of mischief in her eyes as she waited her turn that was rather attractive.

He racked his brain, trying to remember when she had joined the game, or whether he had seen her any other night, but he came up blank. More worrying was the fact that he couldn't even come up with anything on her in his catalogue of tells; it usually only took him a few rounds to be able to know everything about his opponents, but she remained as much a mystery to him as the workings of Owen's radars.

'Your bet, Mr Walker.'

Bruce nodded at the dealer, then quickly scanned the cards on the table before glancing at his own. Bruce nodded at the dealer, then quickly scanned the cards on the table before glancing at his own. It looked like he was going to have to put a bit more effort into playing if he didn't want to end the night as skint as when he'd first turned up at the casino.

He placed a couple of cards on the table. 'Two.'

A couple of replacements slid his way and he slotted them into his hand. 'Raise.' He threw a stack of coins into the pot, then smiled at the woman.

She met his eyes and smiled back. 'I was wondering when you'd start playing properly.'

'I had to, or you'd have had the shirt from my back.'

She raised an eyebrow and dropped her eyes to his chest. 'Would that be such a bad thing?'

Bruce shot her one of his most winning grins. It looked like he might not be as jinxed as he thought he was - if he played his cards right, so to speak, playing poker might not be the only way for him to forget his troubles for a while.

CHAPTER 6

The following two days went by much as the previous ones had. May ended and June began, but nothing really changed. Gwen, Abby and Drake continued to train with the Spitsteam pilots, keeping a close eye on Eulalia and Taylor as they had said they would, while the rest of the pilots worked with the base's ground crews. With so many hands on deck the new aircraft rapidly approached completion and Dreadnought quickly began to look less of a jigsaw puzzle and more like the predator she was.

It wasn't just military efficiency behind the speed with which the work was being done, there was also a sense of real urgency, as daily reports came in from Eulalia's network of spies on the progress of the Prussians. The armoured divisions were being pushed to their limits, travelling almost a hundred miles every day and at that rate they would be knocking on Gibraltar's door in less than a week.

That wasn't the only threat on the horizon, though, nor was it the most immediate, and Higgins called everyone - Misfits, Spitsteam and Nelson aircrews, as well as a few of the senior officers - into the main briefing room that afternoon to inform them of the new development.

He leaned on a lectern on a stage at the front of the room, chatting with Justine Charmers and a couple of the other senior pilots until everyone was seated, then waved them to silence. 'Evening, chaps! First of all, sorry about the cold - the heating's on the blink. This'll be quick, though, so just grin and bear it!'

Someone in the crowd blew a raspberry and Higgins laughed along with everyone else before pressing buttons on his lectern.

The lights in the room went off and an image was projected on the white wall behind him.

'For those of you who haven't been here long, we send a reconnaissance Spit across the straight every few days to take a look at our friends over there. This is the Prussian airfield on the outskirts of Tangiers last week.' He used a long wooden stick to point out the various features. 'There are three fairly run-down hangars for the single MU9 squadron and half an FU88 squadron based there - you can actually see the wing of an FU88 through a hole in the roof of this one here. There are only six anti-aircraft guns around the perimeter for defence and very few outlying buildings. We believe this is a mess, this is a guard room and this is a radio shed, see the antennae next to it?'

Owen coughed, a cough that sounded suspiciously like the word "antennas" and the Misfits sniggered.

'Eh, what?' Higgins asked, shading his eyes and peering into the darkness past the light of the projector. 'Something funny?' He looked to the image and back. 'Am I missing something?'

'No, sir!' called out Abby. 'I just have children for pilots, that's all.'

'Ah!' said Higgins, 'right you are.' He grinned, then turned back to the image. 'Anyway, you'll note there are no barracks in this image. We believe the personnel all live in the city a few miles away - we caught a few buses unloading men on camera one morning. That meant that their response time if we ever raided them would have been a tad on the slow side.'

He waited a few seconds to let the information sink in, then pressed another button. 'Things are a bit different now, though; this is from a couple of hours ago.'

The image changed. It had been taken from a different angle than the previous one, but it was recognisably the same base. However, now there were row upon row of aircraft - at least a couple of hundred fighters and bombers - neatly lined up and filling almost all of the airfield, leaving only a small open strip between them to actually take off and land.

'As you can see, a few reinforcements have been moved in...'

There were some chuckles, but most of the inexperienced pilots and aircrews were just staring in shock at the largest collection of enemy aircraft they had ever seen.

'That's not the only change the blighters have made, though.' Higgins pressed another button and after a brief flicker the same photograph came back up, but this time covered with red rings and other markings.

'There are now *thirty*-six anti-aircraft emplacements, that we can see anyway, and building work is under way to the south of the airfield. By the looks of things, they've laid foundations for about half a dozen barracks buildings, as well as a few workshops and hangars just outside the perimeter fence to expand the base itself.' The image changed as he cycled through several photographs showing the base from different angles.

'That's not all, though. The pilot,' he searched among the group of Spitsteam pilots, 'I believe it was Fanny's turn today, wasn't it, Justine?'

'Yes, sir, it was,' Charmers answered.

'Fanny spotted something while she was making her run and went out of her way to get pictures for us, despite being under some pretty heavy fire and fighters taking off to chase her, so, gold star, Fanny, well done! Top of the class!'

A cheer went up and a young woman stood and bowed ironically to applause and laughter. Higgins grinned and waited, allowing it to die out on its own before bringing up the next image, which showed dozens of big machines working to clear a roughly square piece of land - an airbase in its early stages.

'The Prussians are constructing this second, much bigger airbase about ten miles to the south of the existing one. We can only assume that they'll move at least half of their aircraft here once it's up and running and, knowing them, that'll probably be in a couple of days. So, what we're going to do is hit them for six while they're still packed in like sardines in a tin.'

Twenty four Nelsons, two full squadrons of Spitsteams and three Misfit aircraft began streaming one by one out of the side of the mountain fifteen minutes before first light the next morning.

As the fastest aircraft, the Misfits were the last to take off and, by the time they did, there was a faint brightening of the sky in front of them as the sun prepared to poke its head up. They banked sharply to the right, turning southwards in an attempt to stay out of sight of any watchers in Spain, and Gwen glanced back at the rock. The hangar door was already closing, swiftly blocking off the red night-working lights, but for a moment it looked a bit too much like the mouth of some hell-beast, one that had just disgorged a flock of bats to play havoc with humanity. She shivered as she had a sudden premonition of impending disaster, but shook it off quickly; it wasn't as if any mission she'd ever flown hadn't had at least the possibility, if not the very real probability, of disaster.

She put Excalibur onto the correct heading and squinted into the night, searching for Dragon. The aircraft had taken off five seconds apart, the minimum distance for safety in the dark, so she wasn't too worried about a collision, but five seconds in a fighter, even just after takeoff, translated to half a mile or more and she couldn't find her anywhere. The sky was expanding rapidly as dawn approached, though, and her efforts were rendered redundant as suddenly her vision was filled with British aircraft. She spotted Dragon slightly off to the right of her nose, and pushed the throttle forwards to gain speed and pulled up beside her. Moments later Lion did the same on the other side and Abby waved to them, then pointed down.

Together, the three aircraft sank towards the sea. A few miles ahead, the Spitsteam squadrons were beginning to do the same, while beyond them, the Nelsons were forming up into a solid mass as they climbed.

The raid had been timed so that the aircraft would arrive as soon as there was enough light to see targets on the ground clearly, hoping to catch the Prussians asleep, or at least snoozing. The fighters were going in first and get in at least a couple of clear runs at the anti-aircraft guns and knock as many of them out as possible before the bombers arrived to give the enemy aircraft a good pounding. It was all going to be done in strict radio silence, at least until the enemy was engaged, so as to give the Prussians as little time to react as possible, the fifty-strong British force following the precise timings laid down by Higgins' group of planners. It looked extremely simple on paper and they should by all rights be in and out with the minimum of fuss and be back home for breakfast before the Prussians even knew what had hit them, but Gwen couldn't quite shake that feeling in her gut of something dreadful about to happen. The same feeling she'd had before the attack on Bertha.

She dropped her eyes from watching the bombers bumbling around and looked over her left wing at Africa. It took a very clear day for France to be visible from the cliffs of Dover with a telescope, but the coast of the Kingdom of Morocco was half the distance from Gibraltar and could be seen clearly with the naked eye on most days. From her position in the middle of the channel Gwen was even close enough to make out some details - small fishing villages, ancient-looking fortifications, stone lighthouses, even a huge flock of off-white blobs on a hillside that were probably goats. Aside from the squat, dark grey fortress the Prussians had built on the peak of "Jebel Musa", the mountain which was said to be the southern of the two pillars of Hercules, the northern being Gibraltar itself, to keep an eye on the British, it looked picturesque and peaceful.

Africa was the only one of the seven continents Gwen had never visited. She had travelled the world with her parents for the yearly meetings of the *Société Aéronautique*, but she'd had chickenpox when it had been held in Cairo and she'd missed the meeting held on the slopes of Kilimanjaro by the Kenyans, famous for their kites and gliders, because she'd been in the early days of her relationship with Richard and had stayed at Oxford to be with him. The brief visit during the mission wouldn't count. At least, not if everything went well and she wasn't forced to actually set foot on African soil.

She reached out to tap the wooden panel carved with the name Excalibur that was fixed above her instruments, a superstition she'd picked up from her maternal grandmother, then stroked the photograph of Kitty tucked behind it.

'We'll go there together someday, darling.'

The chronograph on the wrist of her lifted arm caught her eye and she started and looked down at the notes on her thigh.

'Oh sh...' She muttered, annoyed with herself; not only had she not been watching for hostile aircraft while she'd been daydreaming, but she'd also almost missed the scheduled turn.

She glanced to the side to find Abby already signalling and the three Misfits banked sharply, closely followed by the Spitsteams - the entire fighter group turning until they were perpendicular to the land and pointing directly at the airfield.

Five miles to go. One minute until the peace and quiet of the burgeoning dawn would be ripped apart.

Flying a couple of dozen yards above the sea in semi-darkness had afforded the British aircraft some protection from observation, but they were well within range of any observers on the coast now, the light was bright enough for them to be clearly visible, and Gwen gripped her stick tighter, the muscles in her legs and arms stiffening, expecting the anti-aircraft batteries on the coast to open up at any moment. They remained completely silent, though, and the fighters crossed onto land and sped past them, close enough to reach out and touch the barrels of the guns as they pointed mutely skywards. Gwen couldn't help but laugh at the sight of a young Prussian, wearing only a pair of white shorts and a grey uniform hat, standing on the steps of a house near an anti-ship cannon on the seafront, scratching himself and watching sleepily as the aircraft approached, then falling over himself to rush inside, and the tension flooded from her as she realised that there would be no gauntlet of fire to run.

'Typhoon Leader to all Typhoon aircraft. Twenty seconds to target. Climbing now. Happy hunting.'

So close to the target, and having been seen, there was no need for radio silence and Abby gave the word to begin the attack, which called for the fighters to split up into elements and climb to five hundred feet so they could pick out their assigned targets.

Higgins had chosen types of storms for the callsigns of the fighter and bomber groups, "Typhoon" and "Cyclone" respectively, as if expecting that they would be as destructive to the enemy as their namesakes. However, the storm that broke out as soon as the fighters rose from the cover of the ground wasn't one of their making.

Incandescent lines reached out for the aircraft, seemingly from everywhere, as all of the anti-aircraft guns around the airfield opened fire simultaneously, *their* gunners apparently very much awake and alert. An element of two Spitsteams were caught in a particularly intense crossfire and disintegrated, falling from the sky before the pilots even knew they were in danger, but the rest came through the initial surprise and shock intact and began juking around the sky in an effort to avoid the hail of metal while they closed to firing distance.

Gwen winced as tracer fire shot by her wing, only feet away. It passed between her and Abby, going through the space where she would have been if she hadn't adjusted course immediately on beginning climbing - since there were three Misfits and the performance of Dragon was so similar to that of Lion, Abby had decided she and Drake would form an element for the mission, leaving Gwen on her own so that she could use Excalibur's full capabilities and assigning her separate targets. That decision had saved her life, at least momentarily, and she began to throw her aircraft around the sky, rolling and weaving to confuse the gunners as the adjusted their aim.

She was only seconds away from the enemy base now, though, and the violent manoeuvring was preventing her from finding her targets. She risked a pause in her evasive actions, holding Excalibur standing on a wingtip for the briefest of moments, and scanned the landscape ahead. Flashes of light from the muzzles of guns gave away the positions of the anti-aircraft emplacements surrounding the base and she quickly picked out the three she had been assigned. They were just outside the perimeter fence, to the south-east of the airfield, exactly where they were supposed to be, the analysis of the surveillance photographs accurate, the planning of her route spot on, and she swerved towards them and went back to her manoeuvres. However, she frowned as she did so. In that all too brief glimpse she had noticed something about the base wasn't right - there was something that didn't agree with the mental picture she had formed of it from the images in the briefing. She couldn't quite put her finger on what was wrong, though.

Thankfully, Abby wasn't nearly as slow on the uptake and her voice came over the crackling general frequency. 'Cyclone Leader, abort mission. Break off your attack and return to base. Typhoons, ignore the guns and target the enemy aircraft.'

The change of plan gave Gwen's conscious mind the nudge it needed to catch up with her unconscious one and she finally saw what should have been immediately and glaringly obvious - the airbase was almost completely empty. Instead of the two hundred-odd aircraft they had been expecting, there were not more than a few dozen.

'Is it too much to ask for things to go as planned for once...?' she growled under her breath as she banked sharply to bring her guns in line with one of the neat lines of parked fighters. The sight of her cannon fire demolishing a group of three MU9's and another six aircraft being destroyed as the other British fighters joined the attack did something to assuage her frustration at the lost opportunity, though, and she grinned.

'One run only, Typhoons, then break off for home.'

Abby's latest order put paid to Gwen's plans of several leisurely, but lightning-fast, attack runs and she immediately kicked her rudder to slew Excalibur towards a couple of Funkel FU88's parked hard up against the perimeter fence. While it would have been nice to stay around and do a lot more damage to the Prussians, it made sense not to linger too long over the airfield - there were too many antiaircraft guns and not enough targets to make the risk worthwhile - but she was damned if she wasn't going to do her utmost to thin the enemy's numbers before she had to leave. However, before she could get the eighty-eights in her sights, a couple of the guns beyond them singled her out for attention and she was forced to pull up sharply, out of their line of fire. She didn't give up on her attack, though, and rolled, throwing Excalibur onto her back, while dragging her nose back down towards the horizon. The first of the bombers swam back into her vision and she remained inverted as she opened fire on it, holding the triggers for long seconds, knowing she had the ammunition to spare.

Cannon rounds shook the big machine, ripping huge chunks in its thick armour and she grunted in satisfaction. Unfortunately, in her bloodthirstiness and eagerness to destroy the enemy machine she hadn't been paying attention to her own and her heart leapt into her mouth when she felt the first judders of a burgeoning stall - the recoil of her guns had slowed her so much that she was in real danger of falling from the sky.

She reacted instantly, shoving the throttle through the stops into emergency unwind, sending the machine surging forwards as the over-sized airscrew bit the air. The shaking began to subside, but she still thought she was a goner for a moment as she was forced to fly straight and level, a sitting duck for the Prussian heavy machine guns, the hard-packed earth and thin grass of the airfield so close she could almost have opened her canopy and reached up to get her first touch of African soil.

There was a sharp rattle as her fuselage was struck over and over, the noise coming almost continuously, and she winced, waiting for the end to come. However, there was no final and deadly bang, no sudden agony before the Dark Scythesman came for her, and Excalibur remained in one piece as she flew on, her belly to the sky. The sound continued, though, mystifying her, until something struck the canopy over her head. Out of instinct her eyes shot upwards and she finally saw what was causing it: her massive propeller was throwing loose earth and small stones up and it was pattering against her tail section.

She looked towards the guns, wondering why they hadn't blown her from the sky, but couldn't see them and laughed in relief when she saw that she was so close to the ground that the FU88's on the edge of the airfield were completely hiding her from them and they couldn't fire without hitting their own machines. In the chaos of a full scale aerial battle, with enemy machines being blasted apart all around and tracers from the dozens of anti-aircraft guns streaking above her, through a sky which had been darkened once more by clouds of ack-ack, she had managed to find herself a brief moment of calm. It only lasted a few seconds, but it was more than enough to save her life and as soon as Excalibur had lost all her hesitation, Gwen touched her rudder to give the second bomber a burst of cannon fire, a much shorter one this time, then went up and over it. She was past the Prussian guns before they could even think of tracking her and, staying low out of their sight, she finally rolled to right herself, then skirted around the airfield until she could safely head north and speed for the coast.

Understandably, it was a fairly dejected group that met in the sitting room before bed that evening and not even the jokes at Gwen's expense about her unconventional tactics over the Prussian airfield had lightened the mood for long.

'In hindsight it must have been pretty easy to predict what we were going to do.' Derek said. 'They saw the reconnaissance Spitsteam. They know we have a penchant for dawn raids. *Of course* they would lay a trap for us...' He sighed, shaking his head, then looked down into his wine.

'The coastal guns not opening up on you was a good touch.' Owen added. 'It gave them the element of surprise at the same time as it gave you a false sense of security.'

The Misfits who hadn't flown the mission had naturally been told all about it by the pilots who had and it had been the only topic of discussion heard on the base during the entire day. This was the first time they could sit down and analyse it properly, though.

'And it's a damn shame about Taylor.' Owen added.

There were sad grunts of agreement. Three Spitsteams and their pilots had been lost in the raid - the two which had been destroyed immediately by the guns around the base and one more by the coastal guns when the aircraft had retreated - all of them shot down so low that there wasn't any hope for the pilots to have survived. Sergeant Taylor had been one of the pilots shot down over the base in the opening salvo, killed before he had gotten the chance to take a single shot. It was a sobering reminder that even the best of pilots could be taken down in a moment by a stroke of bad fortune. The Misfits had been lucky enough to avoid that fate, but they were all well aware that it could happen at any time.

'It's good that Higgins supported your decision to call off the bombers,' Drake pointed out, 'even if the Nelson boys weren't happy. The last thing we need in this situation is a do or die commander; I've had too many of those.'

Again, the only thing that greeted the statement were nods and affirmative noises as the Misfits struggled to scrape together enough enthusiasm to do anything more.

There wasn't much else to say and the Misfits lapsed into silence, the only noises the occasional slurp and the crunching of the biscuits Wendy was dipping into her wine to Derek's disgust.

'Bloody cheery lot we are!' Bruce laughed. 'Come on, the convoy will be here in a couple of weeks and then we'll be on our way home!'

Most of the pilots stared at him, shocked at his sudden, uncharacteristic cheerfulness, but Scarlet just looked him up and down, then grinned. 'What have you been doing? Or should I say *who*?'

'Well...' Bruce started with a grin, causing Scarlet to lean forwards in eager anticipation and the rest of the pilots to groan. However, a knock at the street door interrupted him before he could make whatever crude or crass statement he was going to make and he had to satisfy himself with merely sticking out his tongue at the Irishwoman as he leapt to his feet and jogged out to answer it.

He was back in only a few seconds with Vice-Marshal Higgins in tow.

'Good evening, everybody.'

'Evening, sir. Would you like a drink?' Abby motioned at the collection of bottles on the side table, which seemed to grow daily.

Higgins smiled and shook his head. 'Very kind, but no, thank you; I won't be staying. I just popped by to let you know that we managed to get in touch with Alexandria today for the first time in months - the wind was in the right direction or something.' He waved his hand vaguely. 'I don't really understand these things. Anyway, they're having a devil of a time of it down in Alex right now, what with the Prussians on all sides. They're doing what they can to hold them off while they evacuate, but it's not looking good. Anyway, it seems a friend of yours is helping them out at the moment, uh, sorry, her name's slipped my mind. It's something unusual, though,' he frowned, 'Charity, is it? Or Chatterley?'

'Chastity?' asked Abby.

'That's the one!' said Higgins. 'Apparently she bailed out and was picked up by an undersea boat. She spent a fair amount of time in the water and was a bit worse for wear, but they nursed her back to health and now she's leading what few aircraft they have in the defensive efforts.'

'Good on her!' Owen called out, over the cheers of the rest of the Misfits.

Higgins grinned as he looked around the celebrating pilots. 'Well, just thought you'd like to know. God knows we all needed a bit of good news after this morning's showing, what?'

He nodded to Abby, then started to go. Bruce made to go with him, but he waved him away. 'Don't worry, I'll show myself out. See you all tomorrow! Good night!'

He waved cheerfully, then left the room, closing the door behind him.

'Well, *I* think that calls for another drink,' said Bruce, grabbing one of the several whisky bottles.

The Misfits cheered again and there was a rush to fill glasses so that toasts could be drunk in honour of a friend they had thought dead.

CHAPTER 7

Gwen pounded down the middle of the street, not caring how silly she must have looked waddling along in her flightsuit at top speed or that she was drawing amused glances from the few men and women out and about at dawn. She was puffing for breath and her legs were like jelly, but she was unwilling to slow down; she had somewhere she needed to be and she needed to be there as soon as she possibly could.

The Misfits had been ready to go on another training flight when the call had come in. They had been doing several each day, with or without the Spitsteam squadrons, but this was to have been the first with the newly completed aircraft and the repaired Dreadnought. Despite the importance of the flight and the dwindling opportunities to train with the Prussians only two hundred miles away, Abby had given her permission to leave and she had left Excalibur in the hands of her fitters and sprinted straight to the lift, which she had cursed repeatedly for not descending fast enough, and had been running ever since.

Now, though, even though it had been downhill the entire way, she was beginning to flag and her feet were killing her; flying boots weren't designed for walking, let alone running. The hospital was only a couple of streets away, though, so she forced herself to keep hobbling along.

She burst through the doors and slipped as her smooth-soled boots lost traction on the marble floor for a moment, but managed to prevent herself from falling and staggered over to the first person in a medical uniform that she could see - an orderly pushing a cart piled with bandages.

'The evacuees from Malta,' she panted at him, 'the ones from the undersea boat. Where are they?'

The poor young man was startled at being accosted so rudely and abruptly and shrank back, but pointed towards a door at the side. 'In there, ma'am. In triage.'

Gwen ran to the door, calling out a thank you over her shoulder without slowing and barged her way through it, almost knocking over another medical orderly, who was on her way out, as she did.

'Sorry!'

'Gwen?'

Gwen skidded to a halt and turned to stare at the woman she'd as good as flattened, taking in the fair hair poking out from beneath her uniform cap and the freckles liberally scattered across her cheeks and nose, then surged forwards to wrap her arms around her. 'Polly! I'm so glad you're alive! I looked for you after the Arturo went down and when I couldn't find you...'

Polly squeezed Gwen back, but quickly pulled away and grinned at her. 'I volunteered to stay behind in the hospital on Malta, but never mind that; we can catch up later. Come on,' she reached out to grab Gwen's hand. 'I know why you're really here.'

The young woman pulled her down the aisle of the long, thin ward, between the metal-framed beds. Most of the beds were unoccupied, their light green sterile sheets pristine, but a couple were curtained off to give privacy to the doctors working on the groaning and moaning men and women within, victims of the accidents that inevitably happen on active duty, even away from combat. However, the beds at the other end of the room, almost fifty yards away, were almost filled by a large group of a couple of dozen patients in white pyjamas, who were being bustled around by doctors, nurses and note-taking administrative staff. Gwen scanned them intently, but the woman she was looking for wasn't among them and her stomach dropped when Polly pulled her past them towards a single curtained-off bed next to the far door.

'Why is she isolated? Is she alright?'

'Yes, of course she is! She's fine! Don't worry!' The wide smile that had been plastered on Polly's face since Gwen had run into her faded slightly. 'She's just, well, let's just say she's a bit less recovered than the others who came in this morning.'

Gwen frowned, wondering what she meant, but there was no chance to ask her because they were at the bed and Polly was pulling her through the curtain.

It was much darker inside the tiny space, the thick curtains blocking most of the light from beyond, and it took a moment for Gwen's eyes to adjust, but when they did her hands went to her mouth to cover her gasp at the sight of the woman lying on the bed.

If Gwen hadn't known Kitty so well she might not have recognised her. She was painfully thin, the arms resting on the sheets on either side of her like sticks, the skin of her face pulled tightly across her skull and the dark around her eyes giving her a cadaverous look. Her skin itself, usually the light tan colour of someone who enjoyed being outdoors, was a deathly white and dry as parchment and the lush golden hair that Gwen so loved to twirl around her fingers was lank and dull.

She looked like a corpse, and if it hadn't been for the fact that a faint wheezing sound was coming from her as her chest moved up and down, Gwen would have thought she was dead.

This was the third or fourth undersea boat that had come from Malta, bringing groups of the patients who had been left behind in the hospital in Valletta. Gwen had asked after Kitty every time, but the answer had always been the same: that she wouldn't travel until she was well enough to survive the trip and that it would be months before she would be.

By all rights, Kitty should still be in bed in Valletta - she certainly didn't look like she should have been moved - but there she was, looking like death warmed up. It didn't make sense, but that didn't matter one bit; all that mattered was that she was there.

'Kitty...' The word was barely audible as a vast range of conflicting emotions threatened to overcome Gwen, but the American moaned at the sound and shifted, frowning in pain.

'Uhhh, what is it now Polly? I've got enough pillows, I'm not hungry and yes, I've been to the toilet... Can I just get some sleep, please?'

Kitty's voice was rough, with no force behind it and she wheezed for breath between every other word, but Gwen sagged in relief when she heard the humour in it, recognising the person she had come to love and rely on, the woman who she had felt lost and directionless without since leaving Malta.

'Kitty.' Gwen tried again and this time managed to get the name out with sufficient force.

Kitty's eyes fluttered, struggling to open, but they eventually focussed on Gwen and a smile broke out on her face, making her almost seem like her old self.

'Hi.'

'"Hi" yourself!' Gwen started forward, but hesitated and looked down at the woman's body, taking in the swathes of bandages wrapped around her torso and the large lump of them under the bedsheets, around her right thigh. She was unsure what she could touch that wouldn't cause the American pain.

Kitty's eyes twinkled. 'Oh, just come here!'

'Are you sure? Your injuries...'

'The doctors have already poked and prodded me half to death. A kiss and a cuddle is a much more fun way of getting hurt.'

Gwen didn't need telling again. She surged forwards and bent down to kiss her.

Kitty kissed her back, but the hands that came up to hold her had no strength in them and Gwen pulled away after only a few seconds and gazed into her eyes, tentatively lifting a hand to cup the side of her face.

'Oh, Kitty. You...'

'Look bloody awful, I know. But I'm healing fine. I just keep tearing out my stitches. That's all.'

'Tearing your...' Gwen frowned. 'Why...? How...?'

Kitty chuckled weakly. 'I'll tell you later, when I have the energy.'

Gwen nodded. 'I want to know everything.'

'And you will.' She stroked Gwen's cheek, then pushed the hair away from her face and ran a finger along the pink line on her forehead, which was all that remained of the fairly deep wound caused by a piece of shrapnel. 'This is healing nicely.'

'The doctors gave me some cream to put on it and I've been taking care of it.' Gwen smiled. 'I didn't want you breaking up with me because I was disfigured.'

'Oh, darling, I wouldn't do that. *You* might, though, once you see what a mess they made of my leg.'

Gwen frowned and looked down. 'It's going to be alright, isn't it? You'll still be able to fly?'

Kitty smiled. 'Yes, I'll be able to fly. And walk as well. Although I might limp a bit and I probably won't enjoy the damp weather in Britain, but then again who does?'

Gwen laughed at the joke, but it turned into a sob and suddenly she couldn't keep the tears back any longer. She doubled over, her head in her hands and wailed as everything she'd kept bottled up for weeks came pouring out all at once. 'I thought I'd lost you!'

Kitty reached out and weakly tugged at Gwen until she laid down next to her, pulling her in close to comfort her. 'You won't get rid of me that easily, darling.'

Gwen had no idea how long it took, but eventually she recovered enough to stop crying and when Kitty reached across her to get a tissue from a box beside the bed she accepted it and sat up to blow her nose loudly.

Kitty laughed softly. 'There's that delicate, refined lady I'd fallen in love with.'

Gwen poked her tongue out and took another tissue to wipe her eyes.

Kitty waited for her to finish, then pulled her back down, turning her to face her. As she gazed into Gwen's eyes her hand stroked down her body, her touch so light that it could barely be felt through the flightsuit. 'Mmm, I've missed seeing you in leather.'

Gwen shook her head in exasperation. 'Stop that! You're going to get me all hot and bothered and you're in no fit state to follow through on the promises you're making!'

Kitty pouted, but the roaming hand stopped what it was doing and came to rest on Gwen's hip. 'What are you doing here anyway, darling? You should have been back in England by now.'

'Didn't you hear about the Arturo?'

'I've been unconscious, underground, or under the sea for the last couple of weeks. I haven't heard anything about anything.'

'She was sunk by undersea boats just before we got here.'

'Is everyone alright?'

Gwen grimaced. 'The squadron made it off alright, but a lot of others didn't.'

'Did Hewer make it?'

'Yes. But Billy Simkin didn't.'

'Oh...' Kitty sighed, saddened at the loss of the young midshipman who had shown the Misfits around the Arturo when they'd first boarded her.

'He went a hero, though, making sure that the men and women of his section got out. He'll get a gong for sure, maybe even the Victoria Medal.'

'Yeah,' said Kitty bitterly, 'another family that will get a chunk of metal instead of their child back.'

'Let's not think about that now, please,' pleaded Gwen, snuggling into Kitty's side. 'We're still alive and together again and that's all that matters.'

Kitty smiled down at her. 'OK.'

They lapsed into silence and just held each other, not needing to actually put into words how much they had missed the other.

Unfortunately, though, a patient in Kitty's condition wasn't going to be left alone for very long, especially after just arriving at the hospital, and they looked up as a doctor pushed his way through the curtain, his head down, consulting a clipboard.

'Good morning, Miss Wright, I'm Doctor Bear. I have the results of...' He stopped abruptly when he glanced up and saw them for the first time. 'Oh, I'm sorry.'

'Don't worry, Doc,' said Kitty with a grin. 'You're not interrupting much. Unfortunately.'

'Oh, right.' The man blushed and the two women laughed, but not unkindly.

Gwen peeled herself from Kitty's side and sat up, groaning as the muscles in her legs protested the abuse she'd put them through.

Kitty chuckled and Gwen smiled down at her; despite same-sex relationships being accepted by society and everyone who mattered to them - the RAC, the squadron, Gwen's parents - Gwen would still try to avoid even the possibility of causing offence to anyone and often pulled away from Kitty if anyone showed the slightest sign of surprise or shock.

Kitty stroked her back fondly, then looked at the doctor. 'So, what's the word, Doc? Am I going out the front door or the back?'

The Doctor smiled. 'Oh, the front door. Definitely. I want to run a couple more tests and keep you here for observation today, but I don't see any reason why you can't be discharged as early as tomorrow.' He looked to Gwen then back again. 'As long as you don't do anything too, ahem, *strenuous*, you take a wheelchair with you *and use it*, and you come back every day to have your dressings changed and your wounds checked.'

Kitty grinned. 'Sounds great, Doc. And can I go back to flying tomorrow too?'

'Don't push it, Officer Wright!' The doctor shook his head in exasperation as he hung the clipboard on the end of the bed. 'Someone will come and get you for those tests soon. Your visitor can stay until then, but then they have to go, sorry; I'm prescribing you an hour in a deckchair in the roof garden this afternoon to get some sunshine, but the rest of the day I want you resting and eating. And you are to do the same every day until I tell you to stop!' He grinned. 'You *will* relax for the next few weeks and that's an order, Aerial Officer!'

'Aye aye, sir!' Kitty gave the man a Royal Navy style salute and he laughed.

'See you soon, Officer Wright. Lieutenant.' He nodded at Gwen then pushed his way back out of the curtain.

Polly had come in behind the doctor and she grinned at them. 'It's so good to see you two back together again.'

'Thanks to you,' said Kitty. She smiled warmly at the young woman, then looked up at Gwen. 'If it hadn't been for Polly I would have been left behind on Malta and taken prisoner.'

'I thought you were safely underground?'

Polly nodded. 'We were, until the Prussians started digging for some reason, then we had to get out of there sharpish. And it was Kitty who got herself out, I had nothing to do with it.'

Gwen frowned; for some reason Polly looked ashamed of herself, despite what Kitty had said. Something must have happened on Malta, but the young woman obviously didn't want to talk about it so she didn't push for answers. Instead she stood and went to put an arm around her. 'I'm sorry about Billy. I know you two were close.'

'Thank you.' Polly squeezed her back, then looked from her to Kitty and back again. 'I know they've already held a memorial service for the Arturo's crew, but Billy wouldn't have enjoyed that as his sendoff; it would have been far too stiff and formal for him, he would have hated it, so I'm going to sort out some drinks with friends of his as soon as I've settled in. We'll have far too much to eat and drink and be far too loud and I'd like it if you two were there. He thought very highly of you both and would have been tickled by the thought of you joining us in crying over him.'

Gwen shared a glance with Kitty, who nodded. 'We'll be there.'

'Thank you.' Polly smiled gratefully. She gave Gwen another squeeze, then pulled away and began to move to the curtain. 'Well, I'd love to stay and be a third cog for a bit longer, but I'm sorry, I really have to go; I was supposed to report to the admiral's office half an hour ago - that's where I was going when you ran into me.'

'Quite literally.' Gwen said to Kitty.

Polly tittered. 'Most physical contact I've had in weeks! See you both later!' She blew them each a kiss, then disappeared.

Gwen returned to the bed and lay back down beside Kitty. 'Where were we?'

'Well...' Kitty lifted her hand to caress Gwen again, but retracted it with a start when the curtains around the bed were flung back to reveal two men pushing a gurney. She sighed. 'I think we were right about here...'

As soon as Kitty was lifted into the gurney and wheeled out, Gwen was shooed away by a smiling, but insistent, nurse and she made her way out of the hospital. Abby had told her to be back after breakfast, in time for the second flight of the day. That was at least a couple of hours away, but she decided to return to the base anyway, walking up the hill stiff-legged and far slower than before. However, instead of waiting for the others in the mess or the ready room, she collected her helmet from the changing room and went up to the gun deck.

The Misfits had been on Gibraltar for several weeks, but the men and women stationed there still weren't tired of making their way up to top of the Rock to watch them train. It had become one of the most popular pastimes, in fact, despite the sudden lack of free time with the amount of preparations under way to meet the approaching Prussians. Some brought picnics, others just a bottle or two, a few had cameras and one man even carted up a small motion-picture camera with him, with what looked like home-made lenses sprouting from it. Many watched with the naked eye, but others shared binoculars, or passed around nautical telescopes and one prim-looking senior naval officer even brought along some tiny golden opera glasses on a stick whenever she turned up, as if she were at Covent Garden.

That morning there were several hundred people on the small plateau, only a couple of dozen of whom were there to work on the guns. It was a much bigger crowd than usual for so early in the morning, drawn by the news that not only would the new Misfit fighters be flying for the first time, but so would the restored Dreadnought.

There were plenty of whispers and looks shot in Gwen's direction as she made her way across the summit, but she ignored them and went straight to the safety rail and looked out over the sea.

The sun was a blazing ball, not far above the horizon, casting a brilliant trail on the calm Mediterranean. There was not a single cloud to share the bright blue sky with the British machines as they flew a couple of miles away to the south-east, only a few thousand feet higher than the summit of the Rock. They were in plain view of their audience, but Gwen lowered the lenses of her helmet, wanting to get a better look.

Dreadnought was describing deceptively lazy circuits in the air while Hummingbird flitted around her and Gwen could easily imagine

Wendy in her cockpit, testing her engines and systems as seriously as she could while simultaneously cursing at Scarlet for distracting her. The huge aircraft was certainly an impressive sight and was understandably drawing the most attention as it occasionally sprayed fire, seemingly at random, as Wendy tested her multifarious weapons, but it was Wolf, Kite and Wraith, that Gwen had come to watch.

The crews had worked on the three new fighters day and night since the Prussian column had been reported, desperately trying to get them ready before it arrived and finally completing them late the evening before. Their valiant efforts had been rendered rather redundant, though, because the news had come only hours later that the enemy had slowed their headlong charge and were now only advancing fifty miles each day, instead of the almost two hundred they had been covering previously. Eulalia said that was because the roads got a lot worse south of the new capital, Madrid, rather than being out of any tactical consideration, but, whatever the reason, there was no longer any rush. That didn't matter to Abby one bit. She didn't want to waste any time whatsoever and had scheduled their first flight for the crack of dawn, even if that meant the crews didn't have time to paint the aircraft properly and they were still an ugly dull grey, with just a coating of primer to cover their Duralumin.

Of the three, it was Derek's machine Gwen was most interested in, the performance of the other two being already quite familiar. She quickly got the impression that Kite wasn't a particularly tight turner, that she would be the equal of an MU9, but probably outclassed by an HH190. However, she seemed to more than compensate for that lack by having impressive acceleration, especially in a dive, and would likely be able to outpace just about anything, which would give Derek the ability to open up enough distance to be able to turn and face any Prussian he got into a fight with. It was an interesting adaptation of B flight's tactics to the new squadron tactical philosophy and would bear more observation and consideration. She was finding it increasingly hard to concentrate, though, because her thoughts kept drifting back to Kitty and after another ten minutes, during which she watched the aircraft without really seeing them, she gave up and made her way back down to the air base.

CHAPTER 8

Even though they all trooped down to the hospital together as soon as they got off duty, the Misfits weren't allowed to see Kitty that night. Neither could they see her the next morning, because they were back in the air before visiting hours. She was sitting in a clockwork wheelchair at the side of the hangar waiting for them when they landed from their flight, though, and she came scooting towards them as they clambered from their aircraft.

Gwen waved as she hopped down from Excalibur and started towards her, but she was one of the furthest away and most of the other pilots beat her to the smiling Kitty, blocking her off.

Eulalia had been flying with the Misfits that morning, as she did most days, and she wandered up to Gwen. 'What's happening? Why so much noise?'

Gwen was too busy trying to peer around the other pilots to look at her. 'We had to leave one of our pilots on Malta because she was too injured to come with us. She was brought in by undersea boat yesterday.'

'Ah! So this is a happy reunion!'

'Yes. Now that Kitty is here we're only missing one of our pilots...'

'Kitty?' Eulalia interrupted, her hand suddenly clamping painfully down on Gwen's arm, making her wince. 'Do you mean Kitty Wright?' She barely waited for Gwen's nod before squealing girlishly and pushing her way through the Misfits, doing what Gwen had wanted, but been too polite, to do.

Kitty looked startled for a moment as the Spanish woman barrelled towards her, but then her already huge smile widened. 'Laia! You're alive! How...?'

Whatever she was about to say was cut off as Eulalia bent down and kissed her full on the lips.

The pilots were shocked into silence by the manoeuvre and as the kiss went on the quiet became more and more uncomfortable and a few of them began to sneak glances at Gwen. She didn't notice, though, because her eyes were locked on the two women and as the bottom fell out of her world she turned and staggered back to Excalibur on shaky legs to speak to her fitters.

'Hey, hey, hey!' Kitty weakly pushed Eulalia away, trying not to grimace at the pain caused by the woman's enthusiasm, even though she'd been given several painkillers that morning. 'I'm very happy to see you too, but I still need to breathe every so often!'

She smiled up at the Spaniard, but then caught sight of Gwen through a gap in the crowd. She frowned, puzzled, when she saw she was walking away, then paled as she realised what the two of them must have looked like. Before she could go to her, though, Abby was blocking her way, gazing down at her with a wry smile on her face.

'I take it you know Eulalia then?'

'Yes, we flew together in the civil war. She was my commander.'

Abby glanced at Eulalia. 'She didn't tell us that bit.'

Eulalia shrugged. 'Without a squadron I am not a commander, but with an aircraft I am still a pilot, so that is what I told you.'

'She's a damn good pilot,' said Kitty, with a grin, 'despite that Prussian-built monstrosity she insists on driving. Have you still got it, or did you break it down for scrap like I told you to?'

Kitty craned her head, trying to see around the pilots, ostensibly looking for Eulalia's MU9, but in reality trying to spot Gwen.

Eulalia pointed off to the side. 'She's at the end of the line, over there and she's still flying, thanks to the modifications you made.'

'*You* made?' asked Abby. She chuckled. 'Actually, come to think about it, I should have known; they've got your signature all over them.'

Kitty nodded. 'Laia saved my life so many times it was the least I could do. Even though it went against...' she trailed off when she saw Gwen standing behind Excalibur's wing with Giuseppe. 'Look, I'm sorry, everyone, I have to... Excuse me.' She pushed the lever on the armrest of her wheelchair forward and rolled forwards, making more than one person leap out of her way to avoid having their feet run over.

'Kitty?'

Eulalia called out to her as she passed, but the American only had eyes for Gwen and didn't acknowledge her.

She made to go after her, but Abby held her back and smiled gently at her. 'Kitty and Gwen are together.'

'Together?' Eulalia said, looking towards the two women. 'Oh!' Her face fell. 'I didn't know Kitty had found someone. And I...'

'Yes.' Abby nodded. 'And you...'

Gwen pulled the aileron down, then pushed it back up. 'There. Did you feel it that time?'

Giuseppe had his fingertips on the control surface, following through like a novice pilot. He shook his head. 'No.'

Gwen moved the aileron again, shifting it back and forth just a couple of inches either side of centre, doing it over and over while glaring at the Maltese youth beside her. 'There! See? It's minimal, but it definitely catches!' She rolled her eyes when Giuseppe still looked doubtful. 'Come on! You can't tell me you don't feel that!'

Giuseppe shook his head. 'No, ma'am, I don't, sorry.'

Gwen threw her hands up in exasperation, finally releasing the aileron. 'Look, I don't really care if you can feel it or not, *I* can, so get it sorted!'

'Yes, ma'am.' The young man nodded, then turned to his crew. 'You heard the officer.' He walked away, looking very much like a scolded puppy, and began gathering tools.

Gwen grunted in satisfaction and came out from under Excalibur's wing She was more than ready to go to the mess and drown her sorrows in several mugs of tea and a plateful of bacon sarnies, but came to an abrupt halt when she found herself face to face with Kitty. The American was standing with all of her weight on her uninjured leg, using the back of the wheelchair to steady herself. She was looking much better, even though she'd only had one day of rest and medicine. There was some colour to her skin and her hair was almost back to its previous lustre, although she was still painfully thin and there was some definite signs of pain in the crinkling of the corners of her eyes, the pursing of her lips and the way her knuckles whitened as they clutched the back of the wheelchair. Her eyes held the same warmth and strength, though, and Gwen felt her heart skip a beat as she gazed into them, but the sight of the pilots over Kitty's shoulder, or more precisely Eulalia, *Laia*, reminded her of what she'd seen. She hardened her heart and looked away, down at the wheelchair.

'Nice wheels.'

'Gwen...'

'What?' Gwen spat, lifting her eyes to meet hers again, but this time in challenge.

'Please don't be like that.'

There was a new pain in Kitty's eyes, one unrelated to her injuries and Gwen felt almost satisfied, even as she felt a corresponding pain. 'And how *should* I be? After... after...' She waved a hand inarticulately in the direction of the pilots, who suddenly found something else they should be doing.

'Eulalia and I went through a lot together. We saved each other's lives countless times.' Kitty's voice came in fits and starts as the bandages wrapped tightly around her prevented her from taking a deep breath. 'Three years ago we were a couple, *very* briefly. But there was never anything meaningful to it. It was just two people trying desperately to find something good in a bloody awful world. I never loved her, not like I do you. And that kiss was just a very enthusiastic greeting for someone she thought was dead. That's all. There was nothing else to it and there never will be.'

'That's...' Gwen began snap at her angrily, but managed to bite her tongue before she said anything she would regret, the part of her that was afraid to get too close to anyone for fear of being hurt, almost, but not quite getting the better of her. She groaned, deflating as she realised just how irrational she was being and the reason why. 'Oh, bloody hell, I'm jealous, aren't I?'

'Maybe just a little bit,' Kitty said with a grin. 'But that's understandable, given the circumstances.'

'I'm sorry. I guess I've never really done the whole jealousy thing. Richard and I never...' she trailed off, not wanting to reopen old wounds.

'Don't worry about it. Now, come and give me a kiss already!'

'Yes, ma'am!'

Kitty had been very weak the day before and what physical contact they'd been able to snatch had been hesitant and brief, but there was no hesitancy this time and the kiss was anything but brief.

It was nonetheless cut short, though, when Kitty swayed in Gwen's arms and she pulled back in alarm. 'Kitty?'

The American smiled weakly. There was a sheen of sweat on her forehead her skin had a waxy tone to it. 'I think I need to have a bit of a sit down.'

She fumbled at the wheelchair and Gwen helped lower her into it.

Once the American was sitting she recovered some of her colour and chuckled softly. 'That was so good, you knocked my feet out from under me!' She coughed and swallowed with some difficulty. 'I didn't think I would ever say this, but I'm parched and I need a cup of tea. And you should probably be in a debriefing or something.'

Gwen looked over Kitty's head towards the pilots, who were disappearing into the ready room, and nodded. 'I'll be with you in a moment; I've got something to do first.'

She bent down to give Kitty a quick peck, then went to apologise to Giuseppe and her fitters.

CHAPTER 9

Two days later, 7th June, the Prussians were very nearly within range of the aircraft stationed at Gibraltar.

It was also Wendy's birthday and the big woman asked the Misfits to meet her in the workshop she'd taken over in the base after the first training flight of the day.

When they were all there she broke out into song. *For she's a jolly good fellow, for she's a jolly good fellow.'*

The pilots laughingly joined in and when they finished they swamped her, pounding her on the back and wishing her a happy birthday.

'All right, all right! Enough! It's time for my presents!' Wendy pushed them all out of the way then reached under the benches to dig out a .79 inch round for the Anglo-Helvetia cannons. It had a shiny silver tip to it instead of the duller lead or burnished copper ones that they were used to seeing.

'Armour piercing rounds for everyone!' She banged the bullet base down on the table, causing more than one of the pilots to wince. 'These can be fired by the cannons on all the aircraft and will penetrate several inches of armour. A few of these in the right place will make mincemeat of most tanks and armoured cars, but they probably won't do much against the heavy tanks and the walkers, so for them I've had a few of *these* machined up.'

She went to the side of the room and brought out a trolley from where it had been concealed behind a bench. On it was an enormous black gun, fully three yards long, with gaping vents and angular vanes in its long barrel to dissipate the heat it would produce when fired and a huge block at its base to hold the ammunition. It looked fearsome and there was no mistaking that it was anything but an instrument of destruction, one whose purpose was to kill the enemy, to destroy them utterly, and it had a bright pink bow wrapped around it.

She grinned as the Misfits laughed again. 'This is one of my new tank killing guns. I designed them to use the same 1.57 inch rounds that most of the Navy's anti-aircraft guns fire because that way we can easily adapt existing ammunition. I'm going to make some armour piercing rounds for them as well, but in the meantime I've gotten a few thousand normal rounds from Navy stores, so they're ready for you to take them up and practice with whenever you want.'

'That monstrosity is far too big to go inside a wing,' said Abby. 'I take it they mount underneath?'

Wendy nodded. 'They do. They bolt in the same place as the racks for the rockets did.'

'Good. Thank you, Wendy, well done!' Abby looked around the pilots. 'Alright, as soon as the fitters have got these on, we'll...'

'Hold on, don't get too excited yet!' Wendy said, cutting her off hurriedly. 'You can't just go and put these beauties on all our aircraft, then swan off to shoot some tanks; mounting them comes with a pretty high cost. For a start, they're too heavy for most of them. In fact I'd say the only fighters that can take the weight without major modifications to stop their wings tearing off are Lion, Wolf, Kite and Excalibur. None of the rest and definitely not the Spitsteams.'

'So, we'll just put them on those...'

Wendy stopped Abby again. 'Hang on, I haven't finished!'

Abby gave her a scathing look. 'What now? After getting our hopes up I sincerely hope you're not going to tell us you can only put these on Dreadnought.'

'I wouldn't do that to you!' Wendy laughed. 'Yes, I may have already swapped the guns in my nose and tail turrets for these, but no, it's not just me and my Whizz Bangers who will get to have all the fun. Although, if my calculations are correct, only Kite and Excalibur will be able to actually fly with the added weight and drag, Lion and Wolf have no chance.'

'Just how heavy are they?' Gwen asked, staring at the huge guns.

'One hundred and thirty pounds each, all told.'

Gwen gaped at her. That would be like having four people lying on the wings and was far more than a full complement of rockets weighed. She grabbed a pencil and some paper from a desk and did some quick calculations. 'Bloody hell, I'm going to have to stay almost at full unwind just to keep from stalling. I won't be able to stay up for very long at that rate.'

'That doesn't matter too much because you only get twenty rounds and you won't need to be over the target for very long anyway.'

'Only twenty?' Gwen shook her head. 'Let me get this straight. Derek and I are going to be sitting ducks, riding in flying pigs which go two hundred miles an hour if we're lucky, having to dive on our targets because otherwise the recoil from those buggers will knock us out of the air, and on top of that we only get twenty rounds to play with? What's that, a burst of a tenth of a second? If we hit some turbulence or sneeze while we're firing it'll be gone!'

'No need to worry about that; I've rigged the guns to fire single shots only.'

'Good thinking, Wendy.' said Abby.

The big woman shrugged. 'Well, I kind of had too, because if you fire more than ten rounds in a single burst the heat could make the ammunition explode...'

Wendy smiled sweetly as both Derek and Gwen glared at her, but Abby stepped in quickly before they could say anything.

'Thank you for these, but did you manage to get together some rockets for the rest of us as well?'

'The machine shop has been able to make more than enough for about a dozen missions with the available materials.'

'Good. Get everything on the aircraft immediately, please, and we'll fly fully loaded for the rest of the day.' Abby grinned. 'I think I'm going to ask Charmers if she and her people want to play the bad guys and try to knock us out of the sky. It should be fun watching Derek and Gwen bumbling about.'

Gwen growled in frustration as she struggled with her controls.

She'd been right. Wendy's guns *had* turned Excalibur into a flying pig. Usually such a delight to fly, the aircraft was sluggish and wallowing around the sky, obeying her only reluctantly when she tried to do anything except fly straight and level. Not since an error in calculations had given one of her first aircraft a centre of gravity so low that it had tried to roll inverted every time she banked had she felt so bad in an aircraft.

She must have presented a risible sight to the crowds of observers on the mountain, wobbling and bobbing around the sky, but it wasn't until the mock dogfights started that the real humiliation began.

Squadron Leader Charmers had readily agreed to let her squadrons act as the enemy, but Gwen had hardly needed the attentions of the Spitsteams to knock her out of the sky. In fact, the only trouble the "enemy" had defeating her each time was that she was going so slowly they kept overshooting her.

Her rate of climb was just as abysmal as her manoeuvrability, at only a couple of hundred feet per minute instead of her usual several thousand, and later, when Abby ordered practice ground attacks, using a patrol boat anchored a few miles out to sea as a target, the aircraft took so long to claw her way back to any height at all that she would be dangerously exposed to anti-aircraft fire after each run on the tanks.

It was her own stupid fault. Both Wendy and Giuseppe had advised her to reduce her armament to compensate for new cannons, but she'd insisted on flying with her full complement of weapons, wanting to remain effective against any fighters that came their way. She'd thought that, of all the fighters, Excalibur would be able to handle the weight. She'd been very wrong and as soon as she landed she shamefacedly asked her young Maltese fitter to remove all but the two inboard cannons.

However, if the flight had been bad for her, Derek had had it much worse. Kite had been designed to be as swift as possible and had less lift and power than Excalibur. Fully loaded as well, he had barely been able to reach take off speed and had all but fallen out of the mountain. He had then been unable to gain height at all and any attempt at manoeuvring was met by the buffeting of his wings on the point of stalling.

Abby had ordered him to land straight away, before he lost control, but he'd struggled to turn back to the rock or get to a safe height to make his approach. Everybody thought he was going to have to jettison Wendy's guns, but he surprised them all by using an updraught to wheel round and round, like the birds he'd watched for hours and hours, gaining sufficient height over the course of only a few minutes to easily glide into the mountain. He had immediately had his fitters remove most of his guns, taking away the two cannons and four machine guns in Kite's wings and leaving just the single cannon which shot through his nose cone.

The second flight with reduced weight was much easier for both heavily-laden machines. They were able to manoeuvre properly, their climb rate was, if not good, then sufficient, and both of them were able to do at least something to keep themselves safe from the attacks of the Spitsteams. Gwen still wasn't happy; Excalibur was acting more like the cows she'd once tried to help herd on the Drake estate than a bird of prey, but she had to accept the situation as being the only way to stop the Prussian onslaught. It was only temporary anyway.

The rest of the day was spent training, frantically trying to squeeze as much into the last hours of peace they had left before they began their campaign against the Prussians the next morning and after a dinner in the mess, which was far too cheerful in that peculiar way such meals often were on the night before battle or when in-laws visited by surprise, the Misfits went their own ways.

'*Buttons, belt buckle, hat band...*' Derek muttered to himself as he walked towards the door leading from the main mess hall to the officer's mess, running through his checklist, making sure every part of his dress uniform that could possibly be out of place or wonky *wasn't*.

'*Gongs, wings.*' He reached the last item on the list just as he got to the door and he paused to tuck his top hat firmly under his arm before pushing it open, even though he knew that, as soon as he stepped through into the room beyond, someone would be there to take it from him.

As he'd predicted, a man dressed in the red and gold livery of army stewards appeared as if from nowhere as soon as the door closed behind him. 'Evening, sir. May I find you a table?'

'No, thank you, I'm here to meet someone.' Derek craned his neck and saw that the group he was there to meet were awaiting him. 'I see they're here already.'

'Very good, sir.' The steward handed him a token so that he could reclaim his hat later, then gave him a small bow before hurrying away.

Derek made his way through the sparsely populated room towards his colleagues, nodding to a couple of the officers that he knew as he went.

'Derek!'

The man facing him, a colonel in the army, called out in greeting as he approached the table, prompting the other two, a naval commander and an aviator lieutenant like him, to turn in their seats to greet him also.

'Evening, all,' he said as he slid into the single empty chair, 'sorry if I kept you waiting.'

The colonel, a portly man in his early fifties waved away his apology with a pudgy hand. 'You haven't, my dear chap; we've only just got here ourselves.'

'What do we have tonight, then?' Derek asked, eyeing the decanters and corresponding wine bottles eagerly.

'Well,' said the commander, a balding sixty-year-old man who sailed a desk in headquarters and whose turn it had been to arrange the wines for tasting. 'We have a young Saint Emilion as our French offering and a rather fine '32 Penedès that survived the purge for our Spanish one. From the enemy side we have a Hock...'

The aviator lieutenant, a woman in her thirties who was the navigator on a Nelson bomber, groaned. 'Not *another* Prussian wine, John! Why can't you bring some Italian, for once? It's not as if there's not plenty of it around.'

The colonel nodded. 'Even Chinese would be an improvement.'

Derek laughed. 'I wouldn't go that far, Bertram, but yes, I agree with Charlotte, the Prussians are getting a bit old, John.'

'Alright, alright, I can take a hint!'

'It wasn't really a hint,' said Charlotte with a grin, 'it was more of a command.'

'Yes, ma'am!' The commander chuckled. 'And to complete our quartet, as the novelty wine, we have a Californian from some vineyard I've never heard of, but which is apparently very drinkable.'

'Which shall we start with?' asked Derek. 'I'd go with the Hock, but only to get it out of the way with so we can move on to better things.'

The others laughed and agreed and, as the day's host, the commander poured the first glasses.

After Derek had sampled the wine, which was actually quite nice, if a tad bland, he looked around the group, keen to begin with the real reason, other than a love of wine, that had brought them together.

'Whose turn is it?'

'Yours I believe, old chap,' said the colonel.

Derek smiled. 'Ah good! I've been saving a cracking good one for a special occasion.'

There were groans around the table at his pronouncement, but they were accompanied by smiles and they all leaned forward eagerly to hear him.

'What if... And bear with me on this one; it's not as far-fetched as it might sound. What if that filthy engine they insist on using in the United Federation of American States was the dominant power source in the world?'

Derek smiled and looked around as his companions considered the hypothetical situation he had proposed, the colonel snorting with derision at the same time as his brow furrowed with thought, the commander leaning back in his chair and staring into his wine, the aviator lieutenant toying with her glass, rotating it slowly in place, a faint smile on her face. The possibility of using alternate power sources was something that he had thought about many times - every engineer worth his name had at some point - but he was keen to hear what this diverse group, all experts in their own fields, had to say on how the world at large would be different if springs and steam weren't so clean and efficient.

'Well,' the colonel said. 'For a start, those contraptions you Misfits fly would be rather different and the war would probably be going a lot worse for it.'

He lifted his glass in salute and smiled at Derek as the other two officers voiced their agreement.

Owen and Wendy wandered along the sea front, arms around each other's waist. It was a nightly ritual for them, a way for them to get some time on their own to talk and continue to heal, if not physically, then mentally, after the ordeal they had been through.

Each night they took their time to walk the few miles to the disused lighthouse at the southernmost point of the peninsula, sit on a rock and look out across the water for half an hour or so, hand in hand, then make their way back and finally go to bed, a little more ready for sleep.

Usually, they would be on their own, but that night there were plenty of people out, doing exactly what they were, thoughts of the coming day driving them from their beds. However, the road along the water's edge was long enough for there to be long spaces where nobody was nearby and the further they got from the mess the fewer people there were.

It was an extremely pleasant evening, the wind calmer than usual and the temperature not quite yet at its summer peak and the two walked slower than they usually did. For some reason, though, neither of them could think of anything to say, so they just strolled along, enjoying the physical contact and gazing out at the ships in the harbour and the lights of the Spanish town across the bay.

'Were you really thinking of giving up the Misfits?'

'Uh huh.' Bruce answered, without opening his eyes to look at the woman lying beside him.

'But then you would just be a normal pilot. And you wouldn't have women falling all over themselves to get their hands on you.'

Something tickled him and he opened his eyes to find her propped up on her elbow, smiling down at him as she ran her fingers through his chest hair.

He returned the smile. 'Is that the only reason why you're with me? Because I'm a Misfit?'

'No... You're also a passable poker player.'

He chuckled. 'That's alright then.'

It had only taken little more than an hour of poker for Captain Perdita Brown to make it perfectly clear to Bruce that the fun and games between them didn't have to be limited to the card table and their inter-service liaison had begun that very night with an energetic, albeit brief, coupling in the lounge of a deserted house a few doors down from the casino. It had continued the same way every night since - an hour or two of poker with accompanying banter serving as foreplay, before making their exit and stumbling a few yards down the road for some privacy.

Tonight, though, she had insisted on going to her quarters, a room in one of the larger buildings on the slopes of the north side of the mountain, which served as army officer accommodation, saying that she wanted to use a bed at least once before things got too busy for them to be able to meet up.

'You know, I didn't do *too* badly before I was a Misfit and I'd still have my reputation to fall back on.'

'Reputation? As what? An Australian?' She grinned cheekily.

He nodded, mock seriously. 'Well, we *are* the chosen people, but I was actually thinking about my reputation as one of the best pilots in the world.'

'Oh, how very modest of you.'

'As you already said, I'm Australian. We don't have to go around covering up our inadequacies with false modesty like the Brits. We *know* we're bloody marvellous and we don't try to hide it from everyone else.'

He winked at her and she laughed then bent down to press her lips to his.

When they finally came up for air she lay down by his side and trailed her finger around his upper body, describing circular paths around the dozens of red scars from his recent shrapnel wounds. 'Seriously, though, why would you want to leave? Isn't it every RAC pilot's dream to be a Misfit?'

'Only those who don't know what it's really like.' He gave her a wry smile. 'Which is just about all of them, I suppose.'

'And what *is* it really like?' she asked gently.

'The papers make it out to be all very heroic and glorious, but it's not. Not in the slightest. It's brutal and it's dirty, and for us Misfits it's been much worse than for most of the other pilots. Since the start of the war it's been *us* who have been sent into one bad situation after another and it's been *us* who have met the Prussians head on every time from the get go.'

Bruce's mind wandered back to the early days of the war, to when the Misfits had been whole and complete and, very briefly, untouched by tragedy.

'France was an absolute farce. We were sent in with the Exploration Force, but we were there more as representatives of the King and Kingdom and were out at a party every night, showing our faces in one posh chateau after another, doing more drinking than flying. It was only when we were as good as overrun and people started dying that somebody actually decided we should probably be in the air instead, but by then it was far too late and we only just got out of there with our hides and rides intact. Our confidence was shot to shreds and we were mourning a pilot, but they still stuck us in the *very* front line of the fight over Britain as soon as we got back. Now *that* was a hard fight and, trust me, you have *no* idea how many pilots the RAC lost that summer because they never released the real figures. Thankfully none of us was killed, but we came damn close, though. Damn close.'

He reached over to the bedside table, grabbed the bottle of champagne they had brought from the casino, and took a swig before continuing. 'Muscovy, though... Muscovy was a *complete* shambles. It was like France all over again, but a damn sight colder and this time instead of pretty decent French blokes flying alongside us we had drunken, insubordinate Russians. Which was just about as fun as you can imagine.' He laughed bitterly and gestured with the bottle. 'We weren't expected to win that one, after all we were only one bloody squadron against an entire bloody invasion, but we did. And did we get any thanks? Well, maybe a little, but not nearly enough, that's for sure! And then there was Malta...' he gritted his teeth as the anger and frustration he'd tried so hard to bury surged back to the fore. 'It's almost as if we were *supposed* to lose Malta.'

Perdita blinked at him in surprise. 'Surely not!'

Bruce snarled. 'The *War Minister* doesn't like us because we're one of the King's pet projects and he desperately wanted us to fail so he can get rid of us.'

'But he wouldn't *deliberately* do anything to harm the country. He wouldn't sacrifice something as strategically important as Malta just to spite the King... Would he?'

'I don't know, but he certainly sent us there to die. As you say, Malta is so important that we should have been part of a huge task force, with multiple fighter squadrons, bomber squadrons and plenty of war ships. Instead it was just us and a single bloody Spitsteam squadron who, by the way, never even made it to Malta. We lost a lot of good people because of that. I lost my best friend.'

He rolled onto his side to face her. 'With Monty and too many of the other original pilots gone it didn't feel like Misfit Squadron anymore, so of course I felt like leaving. But then...' He reached out to stroke her face and smiled. 'It took being challenged by you, even at something as trivial as poker, to realise that some things are worth fighting for. No matter how much they change or what is done to them. In the end, Misfit Squadron is like Britain; it's far more than just the people who make it up and, thanks to you, I've realised that I *have* to do whatever I can to keep it going as long as possible. Even if it costs me my life, but *especially* because it has already cost my friends *their* lives.'

'Here you go, me lad, cop a hold o'this.' Scarlet slipped one of her red tokens into the sleeping guard's hand, then chuckled softly as he moaned and pursed his lips, obviously in the throes of an interesting dream.

She backed away, then padded away towards that night's rendezvous point - directly beneath the barrel of Victor, the more seaward of the two massive guns on the summit. It was a cheeky, needlessly dangerous place to have set the rendezvous, but it would probably be the last time she would be able to run one of these exercises, so she had decided to push the limits as far as she could. Three of her crew, the "students" that she had taken under her wing, were already there and she startled two of them by appearing between them, but only earned herself a wide grin from the third. He was her star pupil, a young man, only a boy, really, who had turned nineteen a couple of months before He loved a joke as much as she did and had spotted her coming, but not let his friends in on it. The other four members of the team arrived over the next few minutes, each of them displaying empty hands to signify completion of their missions to plant tokens on random guns around the Rock. Once they were all there, she nodded and gave the signal to move out.

The eight-strong team split up, four of them remaining where they were and preparing to make their assault on Victor, while the other four, led by Scarlet, headed around the perimeter of the plateau. They moved from cover to cover, easily avoiding the sentries, who were doing their best to remain out of sight, as they'd been ordered, but were all too obvious to the team. They arrived at Victoria in only a few minutes and it was a matter of only a few seconds more for them to climb up the sides of the mounting and onto the barrel itself. Almost four feet wide, it was simple enough for them to pad softly up the gentle slope of its fifty-yard length to the very end.

Each member of the team had their own task. While one pulled a piece of cloth out of her knapsack and another began drawing out a length of rope, the third began to tie it all together. Scarlet had reserved the most entertaining task for herself, though, and, while the others worked, she climbed to the very end of the gun and swung out to hang over the muzzle, using its lower lip as a step. Then, once the banner was ready, the four of them worked together to pass it around the barrel and tie it in place.

Scarlet giggled as she followed her teammates back along the barrel towards the ground, wondering what the army lads who served the guns would make of the signs hanging from them - one of which had the word "*BANG!*" written on it in a cartoonish script and the other "The RAC woz here" - when they saw them at first light. Her team would get the word out so that there would be plenty of witnesses from the other two services, but she wouldn't be there to see it herself. At least if the last part of the night's activities went as planned, anyway.

While the rest of the saboteurs silently melted away into the night, their jobs done, Scarlet picked her way over to the sheer east face of the rock. She attached the lightweight line from her knapsack to a rock, then began her descent.

The necessity of intimately knowing somewhere you were going to be staying for any length of time had been drummed into her over and over at Infiltration and Sabotage School, so, during her time off, she'd scouted Gibraltar and the interior of the mountain, mapping them out in her head. She'd fully explored the deserted accommodations attached to the base, going into every one of the various barracks, entertainment rooms, briefing rooms and such and one of the things she'd noticed was that each of the rooms was ventilated in some way. Those chimneys and ventilation shafts had to let out somewhere and she'd flown Hummingbird around the mountain, looking for where they opened out. When the base had been constructed those openings had been well hidden, so that they couldn't be seen by anyone looking for a possible way in, but forty years of releasing the various vapours of an active air base had discoloured the rocks and vegetation around them and her keen eyes had picked them out easily.

It had been obvious which of the half-dozen holes led to the abandoned rooms - it was the least sooty - and that was the one she climbed down into. Half an hour later she wriggled out of the metal hood over the cooker in the enormous unused kitchen then shucked off her dirty dark grey coveralls, gloves and balaclava to reveal her dress uniform, applied a few touches of makeup in the light of a small clockwork lantern and was ready for the last part of her mission.

The main area of the airbase wasn't nearly as empty as it usually was as last minute checks were made by nervous fitters and mechanics to the aircraft which would be flying in the morning's raid. Bombs, rockets and ammunition had already been loaded, hydrogen pumped into tanks, and lubrication liberally applied to moving parts, but that didn't stop them from inspecting everything again, just in case.

Scarlet sneaked past the activity in the shadows at the back of the hangars. There was no way of telling which of the men and women had been told to keep an eye out for her by Higgins, or if all of them had, so she made sure that nobody saw her - an easy enough task when they were so concentrated on something so important.

The offices, on the other hand, were completely deserted. Nobody in their right minds would do paperwork in the middle of the night, so Scarlet was able to just walk straight through and up to Higgins' door. She placed her ear against it, listened for a moment, then grinned, shoved it open and marched in.

'Evenin', Bob!'

As the sun had doused itself in the sea, sending a trail of fire across the waves, Drake and Tanya had stepped onto the launch which was to take them out to the battleship anchored half a mile from the docks. They had barely eaten anything in the mess - just a sandwich and a cup of tea to tide them over - in fact the only reason they had gone at all was to keep the others company; they had been invited to a formal dinner with the port admiral, Sir Rodney Tipperton, aboard his flagship, HMS Beagle.

From almost the moment they had arrived, the Misfits had been inundated with invitations to dine, drink, dance, or socialise in various other ways from most of the clubs and associations in Gibraltar and also from many individuals, including the captains of every single Royal

Naval vessel in the harbour. It would have been impossible for them to accept even a fraction, so, to avoid offending anyone, they had turned down all but a select few which held personal interest for any of the pilots or came from the few people so important that they couldn't be refused. Even then, they were kept occupied most nights because one of those people was the port admiral, on whose goodwill they depended for a swift and comfortable return to England - if they got on his bad side they could very well find themselves on an ancient and rusty freighter for the journey, separated from their aircraft, or travelling via South Africa or the Antarctic station. A large part of the admiral's duties comprised entertaining visiting dignitaries, though - important Spaniards, who were supposed to be neutral, but were probably spies, and the captains and senior officers of those few foreign ships which stopped at Gibraltar - so while these visits were understandably thinner on the ground than they had been before the war it still meant that the admiral requested the presence of the Misfits at least twice a week, if not four or five, wanting to impress his guests by having the most famous representatives of the British armed forces at his table.

It was Derek who most liked to take him up on the offer, mostly because of the quality of wine on offer, but the admiral preferred to have Drake as his guest, since he wasn't only a Misfit, but also a peer of the realm. Even if that meant he got a rather perplexing Muscovite as well.

Despite these occasions being nominally "formal" dinners, they were usually quite informal, with light-hearted conversation and plenty to drink; the vast majority of the Spaniards and foreign officers cared little for the kind of stuffy affairs that high society delighted in and neither did the admiral himself, having been a common sailor on a freighter before enlisting in the Royal Navy when the First Great War had broken out. That evening was different, though; the guest of honour was an American, the Senator for Paraguay, and the admiral and his political adviser had met Drake and Tanya at the Beagle's entry port and briefed them on how important it was to butter up the guest in the hope of finally bringing America into the war on the right side. The senator was apparently on a tour of Europe, an envoy from the United Federation of American States, sent to see first-hand what was happening in Europe. He had already met with the Kaiser, the Tsar, and the Italian Emperor and was stopping only briefly at Gibraltar before steaming to England to meet with the King. It would be his first and only contact with British personnel before then, so it was imperative to give him a decent first impression.

It wasn't exactly what Drake would have wanted to be doing with the evening before flying into combat, but he knew his duty and Tanya, beyond all expectations, looked to be enjoying herself, playing the part of a Lord's wife well - they hadn't told anyone their marriage hadn't yet been formalised and just let everybody assume it had been. The other guests and the senator in particular, who she had been seated next to, were certainly enjoying her company, her bluntness and honesty going over well with the Americans, who the British had always found "a bit rough around the edges". Her English had come on in leaps and bounds since she'd left Muscovy and she was easily fluent enough to carry on a conversation or enthral all in earshot with one of the many hilarious tales of her upbringing.

After the dinner, when the party moved into the ballroom, the senator insisted on taking Tanya by the arm and leading her in. Once Admiral Tipperton had done the same duty with the senator's wife, he wandered over to Drake, who was standing forgotten at the side of the room watching with not a little bemusement as the American whirled a laughing Tanya around the dance floor, and leaned in to whisper in his ear.

'Damn me if a Muscovite ain't going to do our bloody job for us!'

Watching Gwen struggling like that was hilarious and you should have heard what she was saying over the radio! At the same time it was heartbreaking that Excalibur was reduced to that, though, and I sincerely hope that nothing bad happens to her tomorrow because of it.

Well, darling, I'm sorry, but that's all I have time for tonight; we've got a big day ahead of us tomorrow and I hope you'll forgive me if I want to rest a bit for it!

I hope this letter finds you well and that you still haven't gotten yourself into too much trouble.

Yours, with all my love,
Mum

Abby finished her latest letter to James, folded it in half, then put it on top of the others she'd written since she'd left England and hadn't had a chance to send. As things were going she would probably end up giving them to him herself, or at least posting them once she got home if the Misfits were hurried off somewhere else. Next to the tall stack was the photograph she always propped up there for inspiration while she was writing and she picked it up and gazed at it for a moment, indulging herself. The only souvenir she'd taken with her to Malta, it was crinkled and torn from being handled and mishandled, the faces faded, but it was only one of many copies, so that didn't really matter.

It had been taken in spring of 1934 and James had been ten at the time. He was sitting on the picnic blanket between Abby and her husband, Alfred, smiling that toothy smile of his, his ears sticking out beneath hair that was as unmanageable as his father's. It had been a rare day off for the three of them, with Jimmy on his Easter hols from boarding school and neither she nor Alfred having any urgent business to take care of. It had been a wonderful day, the shadow of war still below the horizon, the English weather unusually clement and food still in plentiful supply.

It was the last photograph that had been taken of the three of them together before the accident a month later that had left James without a father and a grandfather and Lennox Aviation, which had already been struggling, without its owner and chief designer in one fell swoop.

She allowed herself a few seconds to linger over the image then tucked it into the breast pocket of her day uniform, grabbed her cap and made her way to the door.

She paused on the landing at the top of the stairs down and listened for the rest of her people, making sure they were alright, as she always did. Only Gwen and Kitty were home, though, at the very top of the house, and she couldn't hear them. Abby had offered to swap her first floor room with them, so that the injured Kitty wouldn't have to climb up so many stairs, but she'd had none of it, claiming she needed the "exercise". However, Abby was fairly sure they just wanted to be as out of the way as possible; Gwen was very fond of her privacy even if Kitty wasn't particularly fussy.

A frown furrowed her already deeply lined brow as she thought of Gwen. She had been a bit of a non-entity the last few weeks, withdrawing into herself and hardly saying a word to anyone. She'd almost gone back to how she'd been when she'd first joined the squadron, when she'd still been mourning her husband. Hopefully having Kitty back would bring her out again - Darwin knew the squadron would need her at her best in the days, the *months*, to come.

Abby went downstairs and into the lounge where she poured a generous measure of rum, knocked it back in one gulp, then took a deep breath and went out onto the street for the short walk to the hospital.

She had become a bit of a familiar face to the nurses and doctors that worked on the night shift in the hospital during the last few weeks and she smiled at those she came across in the corridors, but none stopped to talk to her; they knew she had other things on her mind at that moment.

The room was dark when she got there, as usual, but she knew her way around well enough to be able to get the small nightstand without bumping into anything and turn the small lamp on. She picked up the book next to it and sat down in the chair by the bed.

'So, where did we leave off?'

She opened the book. The place was marked with a battered monochrome depicting a serious-looking young man in an Imperial Aviator Corps uniform - one of the portraits that servicemen and women used to get in the First Great War to leave with their loved ones while they went to the front. She put it down on the nightstand carefully, not knowing if it was a copy like hers or the original, then dropped her eyes to the book.

'Ah, yes. Here we are.'

Abby didn't particularly like Thomas Hardy and Tess of the d'Urberville's was perhaps her least liked of all his books - she'd had to study it at school and that had turned her right off it. It was Dot's favourite book, though, and she carried it with her everywhere with the picture of her long-dead fiancé tucked inside.

With a last glance at the woman on the bed, who had been in a coma since sustaining a head wound during the sinking of the Arturo, Abby began to read.

'*Phase the fourth: The Consequence. Chapter twenty-five. Clare, restless, went out into the dusk when evening drew on, she who had won him having retired to her chamber...*'

'You do remember that the doctor said I couldn't fly, right?'

Gwen winced as she collapsed beside Kitty on the bed. 'Ouch, that was so corny.'

Kitty grinned. 'It's true, though, I feel like I'm floating around the room.'

'That's nothing to do with me, it's just your injuries. You're still not recovered enough for such, ahem, *strenuous activity*.' It was Gwen's turn to grin as she trailed a finger down Kitty's body.

'You might be right. We'd better not do this again for at least a few months. Good night!' Kitty began to turn away, but Gwen grabbed her and pulled her back for another kiss.

When they were both sated, Gwen padded across the room to fill a glass with water. She brought it back and handed it to Kitty, then sat on the edge of the bed and stroked her hair while she drank.

Kitty finished and handed the glass back, then frowned up at Gwen when she remained sitting instead of lying down.

'Something wrong?'

Gwen shook her head. 'No. It's just... I think I'm ready for you to tell me about Eulalia now.'

Kitty smiled. 'OK. But get back in bed first, I'm getting cold.'

CHAPTER 10

'Five miles to target.'

Abby's warning was unnecessary; several hundred tanks and their thousands of supporting vehicles threw up an immense cloud of dust and it had been visible for almost ten minutes. Instead of moving in a neat column like most armoured divisions, the Prussians were advancing on a front several miles wide, their tracked and walking vehicles doing untold damage to the Spanish landscape, ripping crops from the ground, toppling trees, and sometimes even ploughing through buildings.

Five miles was close enough for Gwen to finally be able to make out the individual vehicles in the convoy, though, and she pulled down a lens and peered at the lead vehicles, trying to find one of the types that she had been given as targets. Ideally she'd like to attack one of the huge Walkers; they were the largest, most expensive and heavily armoured of the Prussian vehicles, but she would settle for one of the "smaller" Goethe class tanks.

'Badgers Two and Four, continue as you are. Everyone else accelerate to attack speed.'

Abby, Bruce, Drake, Tanya and Eulalia surged ahead to draw the fire of the anti-aircraft vehicles, quickly leaving Gwen and Derek behind and she glanced across at him. 'How is Kite, Four?'

'She flies like a bloody kiwi, not a kite, Two.'

'A kiwi?' Gwen frowned, wondering why a New Zealander wouldn't be able to fly, but then laughed when she realised that he was talking about an actual kiwi - the flightless bird. 'At least this is only temporary; if we knock enough of their heavy stuff out today we won't need to keep carrying these guns.'

'We can but hope.'

There was a certain amount of tetchiness in Derek's voice at having to fly his brand new aircraft into combat for the very first time so badly impaired rather than being able to enjoy her full capabilities, so Gwen decided to change the subject as quickly as possible.

'Have you seen anything worth our attentions?'

'Those RAC lenses are that bad are they?' He snorted in amusement, the thought of someone being worse off than him perhaps cheering him up a tad. 'Slightly left of centre, a few hundred yards back from the vanguard. See them?'

Gwen squinted in the direction he indicated. With the awful standard issue lenses she had to make do with she could still only see indistinct forms through the shifting smoke, though, and it wasn't until a gust of wind cleared it temporarily that she was able to see what he had - a pair of Walkers clomping through a field side by side.

'I see them.' She couldn't stop a touch of awe from entering her voice at the sight.

The Misfits had encountered Walkers once before, in Muscovy. In among the tall Scandinavian trees they hadn't seemed so big, but here, out in the open countryside, where they could be easily compared to the other vehicles surrounding them, they seemed so much larger. They had proven easy enough to take down with the judicial application of half a dozen or so rockets, though, and she just hoped that Wendy's guns would do the job just as well.

'I'll take the one on the left, you take the one on the right. Give it five rounds then break left.'

Derek was senior to Gwen, having been promoted to Lieutenant long before her, and had much more experience as an element leader, so Abby had put him in charge of their attack.

'Roger, Four.' Gwen acknowledged.

Machine gun fire streamed from the dust cloud as the Prussians spotted the incoming fighters, but it was far too late to prevent the first attacks, or do much to put off the five British fighters, which dipped their noses one after another and loosed rockets at the larger armoured vehicles in the front ranks of the advance. Several of them simply ground to a halt, smoke and men pouring from them, others blew apart, sending treads, gun barrels and shards of razor sharp metal flying. A couple exploded spectacularly, though, as their ammunition cooked off, sending twin balls of fire high into the air and Drake's yellow and purple "camouflaged" Lion, bringing up the rear of the attack, had to bank sharply to avoid damage.

In only a single run, the Misfits caused impressive destruction among the supremely confident Prussians, but it barely caused a dent in their numbers.

However, it was now Gwen and Derek's turn to attack.

They had live fired Wendy's cannons out of sight of land a couple of times to get used to the feel of them. They had only been firing at the water of the Mediterranean, though, which hadn't been particularly satisfying, but this time they had an actual target.

The Misfits, and especially Wendy, had been looking forward to explosions, fireworks and destruction on a massive scale when they used them on the Prussians. The results weren't quite what they were expecting, though.

Nothing happened.

Gwen was sure she'd hit the Walker with most, if not all of her shots - it would have been hard to miss such a big target. She was even pretty sure she'd put a few of them in the vicinity of the weak point between the driver's cab and the engine block. However, when she craned her neck to look back after she'd pulled Excalibur into a tight turn to avoid the anti-aircraft fire that was searching for the two Misfits both of the massive machines were still marching along, seemingly undamaged.

She scowled. 'Well, that was a bit of a letdown, wasn't it, Four?'

'It was indeed, Two.' Derek sighed heavily over the channel. He had never been one for strict radio discipline, unless he was talking to Abby or over the general frequency. 'I think I saw my rounds bouncing off, but I don't really want to waste what little ammo we have left trying again, so what say we bother a Goethe instead? I think I saw a few... Yes, three o'clock, one mile away. A whole pack of them. Let's go.'

Despite having rid themselves of a good dozen pounds of weight, the climbing rate of the two overloaded aircraft was still painfully slow and they did their best to hide themselves in the clouds of dust as they clawed their way back into the sky, trying to gain sufficient height to make another attack. The other Misfits had been making a hell of a lot of noise, strafing everything in sight to keep the attention of the Prussians from them, but a few of the anti-aircraft guns were turning towards them now, realising how easy a target they made.

Tracers whizzed past Gwen's cockpit, only feet away, and she shied Excalibur away from them, but she and Derek were moving far too slowly, far too close to the ground and she cursed as the aircraft shook, dangerously close to stalling and plummeting from the sky.

'I *really* don't like this,' Derek's voice said in her ears, echoing her own sentiments. 'Alright, we'll use the rest of our ammo on these blighters then split up and head for home. Feel free to spray anything that takes your fancy with your normal guns on the way out, but don't dawdle.'

'Roger that, Four.'

As she followed Derek's slow turn towards their targets she craned her neck around to look at the Goethes. Less than half the size of the Walkers they were no less impressive, towering over the normal tanks surrounding them. Running on four extremely thick tracks, they were basically just mobile gun platforms, each carrying a single cannon that was not a lot smaller than Victor and Victoria.

There was only one way the Prussians were going to get into Gibraltar and that was to knock out the guns on the mountain so that the Walkers could safely get troops across the defences on the isthmus. Normal tanks wouldn't be able to do that because their range was too limited, but the Goethes could bombard Gibraltar from almost thirty miles away, out of reach of all but the two huge guns on the summit. If they could be destroyed before they got into range then there would be nothing threatening the British guns and they would be able to pick the Walkers off at their leisure and more than likely defeat the attack.

The first of the tanks appeared in Gwen's sights and she opened fire, pumping the trigger in rapid succession. Excalibur baulked and stuttered at the recoil and she fought the stick, trying to concentrate her fire on the point under the main gun where the armour was supposed to be thinnest.

Her rounds bounced off the armour, sending sparks flying, but leaving barely a dent. She gritted her teeth and kept firing, though, hoping that it would weaken and something would get through. It was a vain hope and she cursed as the guns clicked loudly on empty chambers before they could do any damage whatsoever. She continued to pour out all the expletives she could think of as she switched to her normal cannons and jerked the trigger, liberally spraying the tank more out of frustration than any real hope that they would do anything.

The foul words died in her mouth as jagged holes sprang into being on the tank and she kept firing, laughing gleefully as her rounds found gas or ammunition and explosions wracked the vehicle. The tank slewed to a halt, spewing black smoke, but it wasn't until the gentle juddering of the stick caused by the vibration of the cannons became a violent whipping that she realised that she was in dire trouble herself - the recoil of her weapons had slowed Excalibur too much and she was in the throes of a stall.

She forced the uncooperative stick forwards and pushed the throttle through the stops into emergency unwind in an attempt to recover before the aircraft fell from the sky. Excalibur's nose dipped alarmingly, as did the altimeter, but the airspeed indicator twitched upwards far too slowly.

One hundred feet, eighty, sixty, *forty*.

She could feel Excalibur's wings beginning to bite the air, straining to produce lift, and she eased the now calm stick back slightly, dragging the aircraft's nose back towards the horizon. She watched the long thin needle on the altimeter, morbidly fascinated, as it approached the twelve o'clock position where it would join its smaller and thicker companion.

Thirty feet.

Twenty.

The needle finally halted at just under fifteen feet and she heaved a sigh of relief, but when she lifted her eyes from the instrument panel she couldn't stop herself squeaking in alarm as she found the massive bulk of the Goethe she'd destroyed looming over her, less than two hundred yards away.

Every instinct she had screamed at her to pull the stick back into her lap, to send Excalibur skywards to avoid the wall of grey metal bearing down at her. Every instinct but one, her piloting one, and thankfully that was the one she listened to. She kept half an eye on the monstrosity in front of her, but the rest of her attention was on the airspeed indicator as she waited for her speed to rise.

Two hundred yards was not much room, though, even going just above stall speed, and Gwen couldn't wait for long.

'That'll have to do. Come on, girl.'

She brought the stick back as quickly as she dared, but Excalibur was still extremely unresponsive and the aircraft's nose wasn't coming up nearly fast enough. In fact, all she accomplished was to make it so the gaping hole of the barrel of the Goethe's main gun was directly ahead of her instead of its burning hull.

Gwen had a vision of flying right down it, her wings tearing off and fuselage coming to rest deep within, with her trapped inside forever and as it came closer and closer, filling the whole world through the windshield, she gave the stick one last desperate, ferocious tug, pulling it back as far as it would go. For a split second nothing happened and she resigned herself to a sudden violent death, but then Excalibur surged upwards, as if sensing that something extra was needed of her, and she was over, with scant inches to spare, and there was only the dust of the vehicles and the blue sky of southern Spain in front of her. She shoved the stick forwards again hurriedly, levelling off, not wanting to have to go through the whole process again, and slumped in her seat. She took several deep breaths to calm her pounding heart whilst staring at the photograph of Kitty on her dashboard, aghast at how close she had been to being losing her after only just having gotten her back. It was only when a line of bright fire shot past the canopy that she came out of her reverie and immediately threw Excalibur into a tight turn and looked around to take stock of what had happened while she'd been distracted.

Much of the view through her canopy was obscured by the dust still being thrown up by the vehicles and by the smoke and heat hazes from the burning tanks, but it was easy enough to pinpoint the rest of her squadron by following the fire pouring from them back to its source. It looked like Abby and her team were continuing to carry out strafing runs, pursued by far more anti-aircraft fire than before, as if the Prussians were finally waking up. Derek was turning away for home, though, his attack done, and she was more than happy to obey his previous order and banked around to follow him.

In only a few seconds she was clear of the front rank of tanks, staying low so that the Prussian guns could no longer follow her, and she heaved a sigh of relief and reached out to tap the piece of wood attached to her instrument panel with her knuckle.

'Badger Leader, this is Buttress. Come in please!'

Any feelings of safety she might have had were quickly banished at an urgent call over the general frequency from the controller at Gibraltar and she waited impatiently to see what bad news he would give them after the rigmarole of radio protocol was done.

'Buttress, Badger Leader here. Go ahead.'

'We have two groups of enemy aircraft on radar - fifty plus aircraft from the south-west, just taking off from Tangiers, and approximately twenty aircraft thirty miles to your north-east.'

'And what do you want us to do about that, Buttress?'

'Uh... Hold please.'

Gwen could almost hear Abby rolling her eyes at the man's inexperience. It wasn't his fault; there wasn't exactly very much for him to control over Gibraltar and he had been reduced to something like an air traffic controller at one of Britain's least frequented airfields.

However, there wasn't much time spare for doubt and hesitation if the Prussians were already in the air.

'Hello, Badger Leader, Buttress here.'

'Welcome back, Buttress. What's the plan, then?'

'Prince and Pope Squadrons will intercept the southern group, but they are too far away to do anything about the northern one. That group is at angels ten and closing fast. Suggest you disengage and head for home with all expediency.'

'No need to tell us twice, Buttress. Badger Leader out.' Abby cut the man short before he could waste any more time and switched back to the squadron frequency. 'Alright, Badgers. We'll break off and head for home like the nice man said, but those fighters will probably catch us before we get in range of Gibraltar's guns. So, Two and Four, stay low and stay fast. Maybe they won't notice you, but if they do, then feel free to jettison those guns. Everybody else form on me and prepare to climb to angels twelve. We're going to try to keep them occupied until they're safe.'

As soon as the rest of the Misfits had acknowledged, Abby gave the order and the squadron split up.

Gwen turned her face skywards and watched the five unencumbered fighters climb into the sky for a few moments, envying them their mobility, but then had to turn her attention back to the terrain she was flying far too close to.

The landscape of Spain, or at least southern Spain, was very different to the rolling hills of Kent she had been flying over all the previous summer - it was more akin to the Scottish Highlands, all sharp hills and mountains, although a lot less green. There were also far more obstacles for her to avoid, because she was having to rise up or bank every few seconds to avoid some spire or other. The Catholic Church had only recently been allowed to return to Spain after more than a hundred years and they had gone on a building spree unheard of in the history of organised religion. Now, every Spanish village boasted at least one church, either under construction or repair, as the new government of the country tried to erase everything their predecessors had done and take Spain back to what they say were her "glory days".

With her needing to concentrate so much on just watching where she was going, it was a while before she was able to spot Derek, flitting through a series of low hills a few miles away to her side, but, as soon as she did, she adjusted course to join up with him.

Ten uneventful minutes passed and the two slow-moving Misfits were almost half-way home, but time had run out - the Prussians had caught up.

'Are those...?'

'I'm afraid so, Three.'

Gwen strained her eyes in an attempt to see what Bruce had seen, but with the RAC lenses she could only just see the Misfit aircraft shadowing her and Derek. Spotting the enemy aircraft, which would be at the limit of *their* visual range, was impossible.

The Prussians closed quickly, though, and the next time there was clear ground in front of her and she had a chance to search the sky she was able to make out the cross shapes of their aircraft. She counted sixteen of them and, as they came closer still, she could see that they were painted a very distinctive, very familiar red colour.

The Crimson Barons were in Spain.

'Alright, Badgers. Two and Four are almost home. We just have to stop them looking down for five minutes or so. Go to full unwind and climb. When I say so, we'll break into elements and turn to face them.'

Gwen watched the large group of aircraft closing with the smaller one, waiting for them to show some sign that they had seen the two aircraft on the deck. Unlike her previous aircraft, Wasp, and most of the other Misfit machines, neither Excalibur nor Kite were very brightly painted and Kite actually blended in extremely well with the scenery, so she was hopeful that they wouldn't.

'On my mark,' said Abby. 'Three, two...'

Abby never finished her countdown, because suddenly the Barons turned and banked sharply.

Gwen's heart leapt into her mouth when she thought that they were diving on her and Derek, but it was only for a moment as the Prussians quickly settled on a course that took them back the way they'd come.

'Um...' said Abby. 'Never mind.'

'And they just bugg... uh, I mean, *flew* off? Just like that?'

'Yes, sir,' said Bruce, chuckling in delight at Higgins' near slip. 'They did indeed just bugg... uh... *fly* off.'

Higgins grinned at him, then turned back to Abby. 'What on earth for? They had you outnumbered and must have known you'd be low on ammunition.'

Abby shrugged. 'Gruber isn't usually so blatantly cowardly, but he does things like this every so often. I'm sure he has his reasons.'

'Oh, well,' said Higgins. 'I'm not going to complain too much at getting you all back safely.' He sighed and looked towards the Spitsteam hangar. 'I wish the same could be said for Charmers' lot.'

The two Spitsteam squadrons, already below full strength after the failed attack on the airfield, had been heavily outnumbered by the fighters coming from Tangiers and their inexperience had showed. Despite starting the fight with a clear height advantage, they had lost four machines shot down outright and eight more had barely made it home. In return they had only shot down three, with another two possibles, but they did accomplish what they set out to achieve, which was delay the Prussians long enough for the Misfits to get back under the umbrella of the anti-aircraft guns of the Rock.

'They're going to need a win sooner rather than later to bring morale back up or we're going to lose all of them.' Higgins sighed, shaking his head, before turning back to Abby. 'How do you think we should proceed? Do you want to continue attacking or sit and wait until they're closer and you can be supported by the artillery?'

Gwen and Derek had filled Abby in on the experience with the cannons as soon as they had landed and the group captain was quick to answer. 'We're going to keep pestering them as much as we can, but we'll get rid of Wendy's guns...'

Derek whooped, interrupting her, and she laughed before continuing. 'We'll get rid of the guns and load up on rockets. We know the rockets work well enough and we won't have two vulnerable aircraft to protect that way. I'd also like the Spitsteams flying high coverage on us instead of holding them in reserve like today, if that's alright with you, of course, sir?'

Higgins nodded. 'Sounds good to me, Group Captain. It's not as if they're needed here, with all the guns we've got upstairs! Carry on!'

He gave them one of his wide smiles, but it became somewhat forced when he turned and wandered away towards the Spitsteam pilots, who were milling around their aircraft, looking like lost sheep.

Abby knew there was a difficult conversation coming so she waited until he was out of earshot before turning to confront Wendy. 'Why didn't your guns work?'

The big woman scratched at her chin thoughtfully as she looked over towards Excalibur, leaving a faint trail of oil. A few of the fitters had been listening to the conversation with Higgins and Giuseppe was already wheeling a cart over to the aircraft in preparation for removing the big cannons from under her wings and she grimaced in disappointment before answering. 'Those guns pack a heck of a punch, far more than the other cannons we use. The rounds are heavier and they do a lot more damage, but they're also bigger and travel a lot slower. That means they don't penetrate as easily.'

Scarlet frowned. 'But if they're that much more powerful then why not?'

'Look at it like this - it's the difference between getting punched or stabbed with a knife. There's a lot more strength behind the punch, but it won't ever penetrate your body, even if it's the world champion hitting you, whereas the knife is always going to.'

Scarlet shared a knowing look with Tanya. 'Now, that's the kind of language I can understand!'

Most of the Misfits laughed, but Derek continued to scowl at Wendy. Despite his enthusiastic celebration of the change in weapons he had been in an extremely bad mood since he'd landed and his voice easily carried over the noise being made by the other pilots, hushing them immediately. 'Didn't you test the bloody things before slapping them on our aircraft and sending us out like lambs to the slaughter?'

'Really? I *hardly* think you were as defenceless...' Wendy began to scoff at him, but trailed off when his expression darkened - Derek might be mild mannered and slender, but he was ferocious when angered, with a biting wit and, if the stories from his university days were to be believed, more than capable of backing up his words with fisticuffs if necessary. She coughed and swallowed, but met his eyes without flinching. 'Yes, of course I tested them! But the metal the Prussians use for the armour of their tanks is a bit different from what we use and we don't exactly have any lying around. Now, if you want to blow up some British tanks...'

She grinned at Derek, trying to lighten his mood, but he just shook his head and turned away in disgust.

Abby sighed. It was understandable that tempers would flare up occasionally with the pressures they were under on a daily basis and had been for months, but they couldn't afford them at that moment. Sometimes she wished she could just order her pilots to shut up instead of having to deal with their idiosyncrasies, but that would defeat the point of the Misfits and destroy them more effectively than the barons ever would, so she resigned herself to playing the role of peacemaker again. 'Derek, Wendy did her best at short notice and under difficult circumstances. It was worth a try, but now we'll move on. As I said, we'll take the guns off and load up with rockets and you'll be able to use Kite to the best of her abilities.'

Derek grunted and gave her a nod. He didn't look much happier, but Abby knew that was probably more due to the fact that he needed a cup of tea than any lingering resentment.

'And Dreadnought?' asked Wendy. 'Are the blighters softened up enough for her to come and play yet?'

'Not yet, but don't worry; there'll be plenty left when they arrive. You'll get your chance.' Abby gave her a sympathetic smile, then looked around her pilots. 'Alright, then. Gwen says she thinks her normal cannons penetrated the armour of a Goethe, but she's not sure. We need to find out, so, uh, Drake, Tanya, I want you to find a Walker and a Goethe and give them a few dozen rounds each, see what happens. The rest of us will keep whittling down the smaller tanks for now.'

'And if the cannons don't work on the Walkers and Goethes?' asked Drake.

'Then I guess we're going to have to hope that Victoria and Victor can do something about them before they start pounding us to pieces.'

Gruber taxied as close to the "palacio" as he could, not wanting to walk any further than he had to. He shut Hölle down, then jumped out, tossing his gloves and helmet to one of his mechanics without a word.

He strode up the stone steps to the wide open glass doors, but didn't go straight in, instead he turned to survey the grounds.

The palacio was more a country house than a palace, but the Spanish liked to call their large buildings palaces; it fit their misguided sense of self-importance. It was a moderately large three storey building set in the middle of a parcel of land to the south-west of Valencia that wasn't big enough for even a nine hole golf course, but it did have a big enough lawn for the squadron to use as a runway. The property had been taken from a local businessman after the civil war and given to a colonel in the army as a reward. The Barons had then taken it from him, kicking him out on his ass. It was only temporary, though, because they would have to move closer to Gibraltar in a day or so, but he was damned if he was going to spend that time in some rundown shack next to a dusty airfield in the middle of nowhere.

He grabbed the glass of wine from the tray Lang offered him and sipped at it while he watched the rest of his aircraft land.

These pilots had been with him longer than most, longer than any except for those with whom he had formed the squadron originally, in fact. But they still weren't used to his ways and they shot glances at him as they met up and walked towards the house. They were probably asking each other why he had called off the attack, wondering why he would give up the chance of killing at least those two Misfits who'd been limping home.

They undoubtedly hadn't realised yet that the battle for Gibraltar *wouldn't* be decided by aircraft. The Misfits could blow up a hundred, two hundred, *three* hundred tanks for all he cared, there would still be more than enough left to overcome all resistance and take that tiny piece of land from the British. Especially once the gates were opened for them from within.

No, he didn't want the Misfits dead. Not anymore. Because now that he had them trapped, *properly* this time, he was going to make sure to take them alive.

Nothing was going to stop him getting everything he deserved. And that parade in Berlin, with the hated Misfits in chains beside him, would just be the start.

CHAPTER 11

The first raid on the armoured column had been as much a testing of the waters as anything else and Abby switched the plan up slightly for the second one. They used the rockets on the heavier tanks again, but once they were gone they turned their full attention to the anti-aircraft guns. Those guns, mounted on flat-bedded tracked vehicles, weren't the biggest threat to Gibraltar, but if enough of them were destroyed then the Misfits would be able to act with impunity. More importantly, though, Dreadnought would be free to fly and then the Prussians would really be in for it.

The Barons didn't show up, which the Misfits, knowing Gruber as they did, had half expected, but, surprisingly, neither did any other Prussian fighters. That left the Spitsteam squadrons with nothing to do except circle high overhead, which wasn't such a bad thing considering the drubbing they'd received that morning, but, more importantly, it also left the Misfits nothing to save their ammunition for, so Abby decided to take the risk and use it up against the vehicles.

Gwen was a lot happier without Wendy's guns on Excalibur. With a full load of rockets, the aircraft was still heavy and had been sluggish during taking off and climbing, but she had gotten rid of them in the very first moments of the raid, blowing apart, quite spectacularly, a couple of the larger tanks. Suddenly, after what seemed like and age, but had only been a single day, Excalibur was once again unencumbered and back to how she was supposed to be. Gwen was back on Abby's wing and enjoying herself immensely, using the capabilities of her aircraft to the full to follow her leader in and around the dust clouds over the tanks, carrying out run after run in quick succession, linking one attack into another so seamlessly that their weapons barely had any time to cool down in between.

Derek was similarly delighted to be unencumbered by Wendy's weapons, so much so that, once flying ended for the day, he invited the other pilots to the officer's mess to sample some of the wines they had in their cellars over dinner, an offer the rest of the Misfits were happy to take him up on. He and Eulalia had technically been on Bruce's wing, but since they were also element or flight leaders in their own right, the three of them had taken it in turns to direct their little group, permitting them to wheel and veer unpredictably, like a flock of swallows, confusing the enemy gunners.

At the end of the last sortie before nightfall, the fifth of the day, there were dozens of wrecks littering the Spanish countryside, but none of them were Walkers or Goethes - Drake and Tanya had failed to make a dent in the numbers of the heaviest vehicles. It seemed that either Gwen had been mistaken about her shots penetrating the armour of the Goethe or the metal had been weakened by Wendy's guns beforehand. Whatever the reason, the Misfits were unable to touch the biggest threats to Gibraltar and it looked like it was going to be down to the accuracy of the guns on the Rock to stop them.

It was the only black spot on a very good day's work and it did nothing to spoil the celebratory mood in the mess as the Misfits sipped at the wine Derek had painstakingly chosen, or, in the case of Bruce and Scarlet, knocked it back like water.

When the initial rowdiness had died down a bit, Abby called for silence. A shadow crossed her face as she looked at the all too few people gathered around the small round table, but it was replaced by a smile when her gaze settled on Eulalia.

'You've fitted in nicely with the squadron and Bruce tells me you did very well today.'

She looked to Bruce for confirmation and he grinned. 'Oh yes! She blew the hell out of quite a few tanks, although...' he gave the Spanish pilot a sideways glance, 'it's not *strictly* necessary to swear in Spanish at *every* single one of them.'

Eulalia shrugged. 'I was just letting them know what I thought of them.'

'You do know they couldn't hear you, right?'

She grinned wolfishly. 'They will hear me in the afterlife.'

Her bloodthirsty statement, made with a voice that was more a growl than her usual low-pitched purr, shocked the Misfits into silence for a moment, but when she sniggered, wine coming out of her nose, they laughed.

'I'm sorry,' she said, waving a hand at them while trying to mop her face with a napkin in the other, 'but you should have seen your faces.'

'Yes, well,' said Abby when everyone had quietened down again. 'What I was going to say was that I think you'd be a good addition to the squadron, if you'd like.'

'Really?' Eulalia's voice rose several octaves to an excited squeak. 'I like! I like!' She blushed furiously. 'Sorry, I mean, I would like that very much!'

The Misfits cheered, provoking several angry looks from other diners, many of whom had already been shooting annoyed glances at them for the amount of noise they were making.

'Excellent! Then tomorrow morning I'll send in the request for you to be given a temporary rank in the RAC so that you can join us officially. I'm not sure if the King will be able to give you a commission right away, but I'm sure once he meets you he'll sort that out.'

Eulalia blinked in surprise. 'Me? Meet the King of Britain?'

'He's a sweetie,' said Scarlet, reaching across Bruce to lay a solicitous hand on her arm. 'You'll love him and I'm sure he'll love you.'

'Oh.'

'That's settled then!' Abby stated to more cheers. She gave the men and women around them, many of them quite senior officers, apologetic nods before gesturing for quiet and lowering her voice. 'Now, why don't we finish this lovely wine, then find somewhere a bit less formal to celebrate properly.'

The campaign against the two Prussian armoured divisions continued another day, with the Spitsteam squadrons still flying guard high overhead in case the Fliegertruppe made an appearance. They never did, though, and with the majority of the anti-aircraft guns destroyed and Dreadnought now with them, the Misfits had a field day amongst the tanks. However, they never seemed to make much of a dent in the numbers, even though they must have left the smoking ruins of at least a hundred vehicles of various sizes in the wake of the enemy column.

However, the morning after that, at first light, there was an enormous boom, like a thunderclap, immediately followed by a second, and those men and women who weren't on duty, along with quite a few who were, ran out into the streets to stare up at the summit of the Rock.

A minute after the first thundering roar, another sounded, then another and the watchers gaped as huge tongues of flame speared the morning sky.

It was a relief that the huge guns on the top of the mountain were on their side, but at the same time their firing meant only one, terrible thing.

The Prussians had finally arrived.

The bombardment of Gibraltar began just before dark that very day.

The Goethes were so far off that there was no warning, no sound of gunfire to presage the explosions that blossomed on the isthmus. Although it wasn't unexpected, the sheer ferocity of the attack was shocking, with the already large detonations of the ten thousand pound high explosive shells magnified several times by those of the mines they set off. The isthmus was almost a mile long by half a mile wide, but earth and concrete was blown into the air over its entirety, creating a dark cloud above it which couldn't settle because as soon as it tried it was flung skywards again by fresh explosions.

Spotters on the summit redirected Victor and Victoria and they quickly honed in on the Goethes. They began to destroy one after another, but they couldn't do it quickly enough to prevent them from carrying out their appointed task, namely to clear a path through the defences for the Walkers and their smaller supporting vehicles.

In less than fifteen minutes of intense fire the job was done and the half dozen surviving Goethes retreated out of range.

The last sight the observers in Gibraltar had before darkness fell was of the massed ranks of Prussian armour coming to a halt, forming up into a line that extended for miles upon miles, ready to begin their assault at dawn.

CHAPTER 12

Every man and woman in the cavernous hangar was silent as they waited for the order to go. No matter whether they were sitting in a cockpit, behind a waist gun, or standing by an aircraft, they were all straining their ears, their eyes turned upwards. There was nothing to be heard, though. No matter how much noise Victor and Victoria were making, the hangar was far too insulated, but they still remained as they were, not wanting to miss anything, should there be anything to miss.

Gwen sat in her cockpit, strapped in tight, helmet on, gazing up at the roof high overhead like everyone else. She was ready for takeoff, her spring fully wound, guns primed, feet on the rudder bars and left hand on the throttle. Her right hand wasn't on the stick, though, it was draped over the side of the aircraft, her fingers laced with those of Kitty, who was standing on the wing next to her.

With plenty of sunshine, decent food instead of the short rations on Malta, and sufficient medicine, Kitty's recovery had progressed remarkably in the last few days, although the American insisted it was Gwen's company that had really done the trick. She was still moving slowly and gingerly and needed to rest quite often, but she was out of the wheelchair already and using just a single walking stick to get around.

'Do you think it'll go like Derek said it would?' asked Gwen in a whisper as she followed some dust, shaken loose by the vibrations, drifting down from the ceiling.

'I'm fairly sure it will.' Kitty said, having seen enough of war on the ground to know. 'In battles this size, individual acts don't matter. It's all about the big picture and the big picture this time is that even if they have knocked out all the mines and traps on the isthmus, the guns on the mountain and the ships will still blow them apart when they try to cross over. And if any of them get through the barrage they'll still have the infantry to contend with. Like he said, they have no chance.'

Gwen frowned. 'I don't still understand that - if they have no chance, and they must know that they don't, then why are they attacking?'

Kitty smiled wryly. 'Because this is what happens when you let someone like Gruber, who doesn't have a clue about these things, run the show.'

'Well, let's hope that they don't have any surprises in store...'

Klaxons blared, cutting Gwen off and Kitty tutted and shook her head. 'All that "Enlightenment" and you British never really worked out you should never tempt fate... Happy hunting, darling.' She leaned into the cockpit to kiss Gwen, then went to the back of the wing and slid to the ground, assisted by a couple of fitters.

Gwen craned her head around to watch her hobble off to join Scarlet, the only other pilot who wasn't flying, but then her attention was called elsewhere as the hangar door began to open, letting in a stream of sunshine, and her headset crackled.

'Intruders in the base. All aircraft, prepare for immediate takeoff.'

'Intruders?' asked Bruce over the squadron channel. 'Um. Where are we going to land if the base is overrun, Boss?'

'Worry about that later, Three. For now, follow those Nelsons!'

'Roger, Boss!'

The Misfits began to pull out onto the runway, joining the back of the long queue of Spitsteams and Nelsons, the first of which were already rolling forwards. One of their aircraft didn't move, though.

'Leader, this is Six. I can do more good here. Happy hunting.'

Gwen glanced over towards the white and grey Wolf and saw Tanya jumping out of her cockpit, tearing off her helmet as she ran towards Scarlet and Kitty.

'Dammit, Six!' Abby said impotently.

'She is right, though, Leader,' said Drake. 'One more aircraft out there isn't going to make much difference, but Tanya in here... those poor Prussians won't know what hit them, especially if she teams up with Scarlet again.'

'Alright.' Abby's eventual agreement was reluctant at best, 'but nobody else wanders off to play silly sods, alright? I want at least a few of us in the air.'

In the time it had taken for the Muscovite to abandon her post, the Nelsons had all taken off, the manoeuvre well-practised, and the Spitsteams were hot on their heels. It was time for the Misfits to follow, with the six remaining fighters in their pairs and Dreadnought bringing up the rear.

'Happy hunting, Misfits.' Abby said.

She was echoed by everyone else as throttles were pushed forwards and daylight came rushing towards them.

Tanya reached Scarlet at about the same time as the slower moving Kitty and they hurried towards the offices at the back of the Misfit hangar together. Before they got to them the door opened and the various clerks who worked there spilled out, led by Higgins, who saw them and came running up to them.

'Saboteurs.' He called out, before he even got to them. 'They've spiked the guns on the Rock and have gained entry through the chimneys in the barracks.'

'For Pete's sake, Bob!' Scarlet swore. 'This is exactly why I didn't sleep all those nights! You were supposed to shut off all those vulnerabilities I exposed!'

'Really?' Higgins blinked at her, perplexed. 'I thought it was just an excuse for you... you know... and me...'

'No, Bob.' Scarlet said with an exasperated sigh. 'Oh, never mind. What's the plan?'

'There aren't many guards up here because we're not supposed to need them, so everyone's getting weapons from the armoury.' Higgins pointed in the direction the office clerks had run. 'We're going to try to hold them off until reinforcements get here in the lifts. Come on.' He motioned for them to follow him, then ran off without waiting to see if they did.

Kitty began to go after Higgins, accompanied by the Misfit fitters who had been listening in, but both Scarlet and Tanya hesitated. They looked at each other.

'What have you got?' asked Scarlet.

Two knives appeared in Tanya's hands as if by magic. She brandished them once, but then they were gone again. 'You?'

Scarlet produced a small bag and pulled out a pair of pistols, which she handed to Tanya before bringing out a third as well as a stubby machine gun. She grinned. 'Enough to get started with?'

'Plenty,' answered Tanya.

Scarlet grinned eagerly. 'Good. Let's go kill some Prussians.'

Excalibur burst out into bright sunshine and Gwen banked hard, following Abby round toward the isthmus. The wind was from the west that day, so they were taking off over the town and the harbour and she could see the ships had moved, shifting their anchorages so that their guns were better placed to add their fire to that coming from the Rock.

She was so caught up in the sight that she hadn't noticed that anything was wrong until one of the Nelson pilots called everyone's attention to the mountain.

'Flipping hell! What happened to the guns?'

Gwen turned her head to look back and gasped. Where previously the Rock had been liberally covered in gun emplacements, both artillery and anti-aircraft, now there were mostly smoking craters, and the two huge guns, which had so dominated the skyline, were nothing more than melted and twisted lumps of metal. However, it was the tattered bundles of cloth that were strewn around each of the blast sights that most distressed her and for once she was thankful that her RAC lenses were so bad, because it prevented her from seeing them too clearly.

'Eyes front, Badgers, we have a job to do.'

Gwen tore her gaze away with an effort, but then gasped again as she took in the full scope of the task ahead of the British forces.

Where before the armoured vehicles had been spread out over a wide front of more than a dozen miles, now they were consolidated and concentrated as they converged on the isthmus. Logically, Gwen knew that there couldn't be more of them than before, but it certainly seemed like there were, as they swarmed like beetles towards the narrow strip of land that was all that separated the British territory from the Spanish mainland. They were still almost ten miles away, but the smaller, faster tanks were advancing rapidly and would soon be in firing range of the defenders.

The full force of the RAC squadrons based at Gibraltar would hit them well before they got there, though.

As they flew directly towards the incoming enemy armour, the Nelsons manoeuvred into a long, flat V formation, like a flock of geese. They closed the gap with the Prussians at close to full speed and dropped their bombs together, carpeting the centre of the advance with thousands of bombs. Most of the munitions missed and struck the ground to send small puffs of earth into the air that were laughingly insignificant compared to what the Goethes had thrown up, but dozens struck home on the thinner armour on the top of the vehicles. Scores of tanks slewed and skidded to a halt or were ripped open from inside as their own munitions cooked off. A few of the surrounding vehicles were caught in those explosions or collided at high speed with the unexpected obstacles, unable to avoid them, but most took no notice and left their stricken fellows behind to continue their race towards the British lines.

The fighters made their run right after the bombers, before the dust had settled, the Misfits joining the two Spitsteam squadrons in a long line in order to "mow the grass" - a tactic they had used before to great effect. Rockets flashed and cannons blazed and another ten or fifteen tanks were brought to a halt, but that wasn't going to do anything to dissuade the Prussians. However, the fighters hadn't really expected to do any more than spread a little more chaos and were well satisfied as they left the ground behind and soared into the sky - their participation in the ground battle was over and now they had to gain height, ready to face the aerial assault that would undoubtedly be timed to coincide with the tanks arriving at the isthmus itself.

Last, but certainly not least, it was Dreadnought's turn to join in the fun. While the Nelsons had to break off and go home for a fresh load of bombs after each attack, Dreadnought was able to loiter above the enemy force, giving Wendy and her "Whizz Bangers" plenty of time to pick and choose their targets. The huge aircraft flew back and forth across the front of the advance, wreaking havoc with her rockets and heavy cannon, so low and close that the last thing many of the enemy saw was Wendy's grinning face in the cockpit. She was still raining destruction down upon them when the call came from Buttress that Prussian aircraft had appeared on the radar.

Oberst Schmidt stifled a bored yawn as he and his men advanced through the empty rooms of the barracks wing of the mountain. He'd thought that assaulting the famous British mountain base on Gibraltar would be a challenge, or at least interesting, but so far it hadn't been. Not even remotely.

And it wasn't as if the peninsula was strategically very important, either, because that would at least compensate a bit for the tedium.

His men were supposed to be used as shock troops, making surgically precise strikes to win the war for the Empire. However, not only had he lost two of his best men over Christmas when they'd failed in a foolproof plan to kill the British royal family, but he and his team had been pulled away from training for their next mission (a particularly risky infiltration of the palace in St Petersburg through the underground railroad lines to kill the Tsar, which had promised to be *extremely* exciting and *gloriously* violent) for *this* - they certainly were *not* supposed to be used to satisfy the desire for revenge of some jumped-up movie star who fancied himself a war hero when all he did was look pretty in a flying machine while the people on the ground did all the work.

Schmidt forced himself to unclench his fists and relax his body; he couldn't allow his frustrations to make him tense up, because that would just slow him down if anything good did happen. It was hard to keep calm and concentrated, though, because so far the mission had not so much gone without a hitch as been completely unopposed. There had been nothing to stop them from alighting on and taking the summit of what was supposed to be an impregnable fortress. What few guards there had been inattentive or asleep, making them the easiest kills he'd ever made. There had been no alarm sounded either, no shouts for help or gunshots to wake the garrison, and they'd been able to place bombs on far more of the guns than they'd expected, so many that they'd run out of explosives!

They had finished the job so quickly that there had been more than an hour left before the rendezvous with the extraction boats, so he'd naturally set up a perimeter to protect the explosives. An hour was a very long time to sit in the middle of enemy territory and he'd been hopeful that he and his men would be surrounded, caught in a desperate action until the timers expired and they had to dive off the side of the mountain, taking to their glidewings again, but nobody had come, not even to bring tea to the soldiers.

Destroying the artillery and anti-aircraft guns on the mountain was the primary and only objective, taking the base itself was never on the cards, but there was so little to do, and the British had been so pathetic in their response, that he'd decided to go ahead and just do it. He called all of his men in, trusting that the explosives wouldn't be found in the fifteen minutes the timers had left, and took them to the eastern side of the mountain. It had been an easy climb down the sheer face to the disused chimneys leading to the living quarters and the shafts themselves hadn't presented much of a challenge either (although it was going to be a pain in the *hintern* to get all the soot out of his fatigues).

Once inside they had moved through the deserted annex slowly and carefully, checking every nook and cranny as they went, making sure they weren't leaving any threats behind them. They weren't expecting any; the rooms were dusty and damp and obviously not in use, but they were too professional to leave anything to chance. It was only when the explosives had gone off and the alarm had sounded that they had seen their first British defender, but, even then, what few soldiers they had come across, searching for the intruders the loud speaker had announced, had been bumbling and inept and had stumbled into his team in ones and twos and died silently.

It was looking like it was going to be a simple matter to conquer the base. His plan was simply to take control of the few entrances - the stairwells and lifts. That would cut the British troops off from their sanctuary and make it so that their aircraft would have nowhere to land except in Spain, where they would be immediately captured. The surrender of Gibraltar would undoubtedly follow soon after.

But then things started to go wrong.

It started off as an itch in the back of Schmidt's mind, an old feeling that something wasn't quite right. Then he started seeing things out of the corner of his eyes - shadows that moved or didn't exactly fit, but which were perfectly fine when he actually looked at them.

Then a two man team he'd sent to check a shower room failed to report in.

He signalled to his men to hold their positions, then moved back to the shower room. He crouched just outside the door and used a small mirror to look into the room without exposing himself. Seeing nothing, he gave a quick hand motion.

As soon as Hans, his second, had swept past him, he rounded the door jamb in a crouch, scanning his sector of the room. Seeing nothing he continued deeper, past the sinks and into the area with the shower cubicles.

With so many partitions to hide behind it was harder to clear this area so Schmidt stayed where he was, covering Hans while he went to check each of the small spaces. It didn't take long, but instead of calling out that everything was clear, Hans motioned for him to join him at the far end of the room.

Schmidt moved to join him, but the metallic smell in the musty air told him what he was going to find long before he got there.

His men were in the last cubicle, red liquid seeping from cut throats circling the drain in the floor.

'Gott im...' Schmidt swore. 'Leave them, we don't have time to take care of them. We'll come back for them when we have the base.'

He led the way back out to the corridor and motioned for his team to continue forwards, counting them off as they went past.

Two more were missing.

That itch in the back of his mind was now a headache and looking like it was going to very swiftly develop into a full-blown migraine.

Higgins and a Military Guard were already handing out weapons by the time Kitty arrived at the armoury and joined the surprisingly orderly queue. Most of the mechanics and fitters hadn't touched a gun since basic training, at least not one that didn't go on an aircraft, and a second MG was giving a few scared, but determined-looking, men and women a quick refresher course to one side. Kitty was pretty familiar with the workings of a gun, having grown up around them, so she had no trouble checking hers over. It looked like it had never been used, like most of the things on the base, but there was no sign of rust and the action was smooth.

Once everybody had a weapon, Higgins climbed up on top of an ammunition crate and called for attention.

'Alright, people! I know none of us expected to have to do this and most of you are terrified - lord knows I am! - but we have to stop these blighters, because if they take over this base our friends out there aren't going to have anywhere to land. So, anyone who's actually got any experience in this sort of thing take the lead, the rest of us, follow on and for heaven's sake try not to shoot anyone on our side!'

The two MG's led the group of maybe forty men and women along the corridor behind the hangars towards the wide passageway leading to the barracks. They were flanked by three fitters, two men and a woman, who held their rifles as if they had at least some idea of what to do with them, but the rest followed in a gaggle, holding weapons gingerly as if frightened they were going to go off by themselves.

Kitty couldn't move as quickly as everyone else and was forced to bring up the rear. There was a fresh ache in her leg, a worrying pain in her side and sparks were shooting behind her eyes, but she gritted her teeth and kept going, determined to do her bit to give Gwen and the others a place to come back to.

The crowd ahead of her slowed as it reached the entrance to the barracks and the senior MG, a sergeant with greying hair, held up his hand for them to halt. She caught up and pushed her way through, moving to the front so that she could better help.

Higgins was there and he glanced sideways at her before muttering out the side of his mouth. 'Got shot down over France in the first show, right when a push was on. Landed my glidewings in the middle of bloody no man's land and got caught up in the fighting. You?'

'Catalunya. A few years back.' Kitty whispered back, without taking her eyes off the MG moving forwards to scout the corridor. 'Right before the end my aerodrome was almost overrun. They were inside the perimeter, on the landing field itself, so we couldn't take off. They issued us with rifles and pushed us out the door. Told us not to come back until it was over or they'd shoot us as cowards.'

Higgins winced. 'That's rough.'

Kitty nodded. 'We lost half our pilots on the ground that day, but saved the base and the aircraft. Fat lot of good that did us, though; most of the rest of us were shot down and killed the next day because we were under strength. Only Eulalia and I survived.'

The MG came back and signalled for them to follow him so Kitty broke off and advanced, her rifle held at the ready against her shoulder.

They were moving much slower now, cautiously, so she had no trouble holding her place in the impromptu advance, but when the MG signalled for them to halt a few minutes later it was a real struggle for her to take up a kneeling position, her leg having stiffened considerably. She ignored the pain, though, blinking rapidly in an attempt to clear the stars from her vision again and aimed down the corridor, her finger resting on the trigger guard, ready to curl when needed, the safety catch already off. She took a deep calming breath and looked beyond the sights to the ninety degree bend about twenty metres ahead. The living quarters were a veritable maze of corridors and rooms, but the only way to get to them from the main areas of the air base was through that one wide corridor, which meant the invaders would have to come around that bend eventually. The six other "experienced" men or women took up positions with her, one behind a filing cabinet that was conveniently placed, but of dubious bullet-stopping ability, another pair in a far too shallow doorway to one side that led to the briefing room, but the other two, like Kitty, just crouched down on the floor wherever they had a clear line of fire. Meanwhile, everybody else retreated around a corner further back, out of sight but ready to come charging in if the small group needed help.

Silence fell as they settled down and held their breath, waiting to see what the Prussians would do. Kitty's fear was that they would lead with grenades, clearing away anyone who was waiting for them, but there hadn't been any explosions from further into the barracks, so, hopefully, unless they somehow knew they were there, there was no reason to expect them to do so.

Her leg was really starting to hurt now and she wasn't sure how long she was going to be able to hold her position without shifting and possibly making noise that would give the game away. However, any thoughts of relieving her discomfort were banished as a noise came from around the bend and her senses sharpened to a point, like they did in the air when she was about to engage the enemy.

Bizarrely, it wasn't orders in German or the clink of weapons, but laughter, *female* laughter, and Kitty smiled as she recognised it.

'Hold your fire!' she called out loudly, struggling to stand up.

The others in the corridor looked at her, startled, and the lead MG motioned urgently for her to get down again, but she ignored him and limped forwards.

The laughter had stopped when she'd shouted, but now a familiar voice came from around the corner instead.

'Kitty? That you?'

'It's me, Scarlet! Are you a prisoner of the Prussians?'

'Don't be daft, woman! They wouldn't be able to catch me! Besides, there's none of them left alive now. Tell your friends to lower their weapons and we'll come out - I don't want to be killed by my own side, at least not this sober.'

The wing of the HH190 ripped off completely as the cannon rounds struck it next to the cockpit and the aircraft went spinning away, narrowly missing colliding with its wingman.

'Nice shot, Two.'

'It was, wasn't it?' Gwen said with a grin. The high deflection snap shot she'd taken, whilst sideslipping using the rudder, so as not to stray from Dragon's side, had been one of the hardest she'd ever attempted, but she felt so in tune with Excalibur that morning that she'd been able to make it without thinking.

The Misfits had raced to intercept a reported thirty plus aircraft in the group coming from the north, fully expecting them to be there, but had found themselves facing only two Flea squadrons, one each of MU9's and HH190's.

Despite being outnumbered more than four to one, they were having no problem dealing with the Prussians. These weren't the veteran pilots that had been taken from Muscovy and sent to Tangiers, these were men who must have recently joined the Fliegertruppe, probably dreaming of becoming a Crimson Baron, or something equally silly, and were being flung into combat before they were fully ready. There were a few more experienced pilots to lead them, but they were unable to do anything to save their charges as they were falling almost as easily at the hands of the Misfits.

It was actually rather reminiscent of how it had been over Britain in the desperate days of August and September the year before. Only now the shoe was firmly on the other foot.

'Pete! Bail out! Bail out!'

Charmers watched her wingmate spinning away, his wing gone. She could see him struggling to open the canopy, but it was no good, the G forces were too much for him to deal with and even as she watched he slumped against the side of his cockpit, unconscious.

She grimaced and tore her eyes away from her doomed friend, then looked towards the fight - the red nosed MU9 that had shot him down was there, somewhere in the melee, and she would dearly love to pay him back for what he had done if she had the chance.

While the Misfits had gone north, she and her two squadrons had been sent to face the southern group once more. It was far larger than before, though, comprising of more than a hundred aircraft, the Prussians feeling safe enough to send their bombers over from Africa after the attack on the anti-aircraft guns on the mountain.

As she circled back towards the main group of aircraft she had a few seconds to assess the situation.

Things were going quite badly. They had been sent with the express purpose of deterring the bombers, but her pilots were so grossly outclassed by the fighters that they were having to concentrate more on not dying than doing their job.

There was no way they were going to be able to do anything to protect Gibraltar on their own. They needed help and there was only one place that was going to come from.

She switched her radio over to the general frequency. 'Badger Leader, this is Prince Leader, requesting assistance.'

'Three, Five, disengage when you can and take your elements to support Prince.'

'Roger, Leader.'

'Got it, Boss.'

'Two, we have to keep these blighters off their backs. Split up and let's give them something to worry about.'

'With pleasure, Leader.'

Gwen was thrust down in her chair by extreme G forces as she immediately broke off from Abby, pulling a turn far tighter than any of the pursuing Prussians, or even Dragon, could manage.

She grinned through the strain of keeping herself conscious. 'Right, then! Now we can *really* start flying.'

Charmers weaved and rolled desperately, trying to escape the fighters on her tail, but no matter what she did they stayed with her. Tracers flew past her Spit over and over as they tried their luck, but so far nothing had hit her. They were getting a lot closer, though, and she was starting to get very tired, her arms aching with the effort of pulling the aircraft around the sky. There was no way she was going to be able to hold them off for much longer.

'Damn those Misfits, where the...'

She flinched as two aircraft, one grey, the other brown and white, appeared from out of nowhere and flew past her on either side, impossibly close and impossibly fast, points of light winking along their wings. She craned her head as she pulled into a turn to follow them and saw both the MU9's that had been chasing her literally fall apart in the air.

'Need a hand, Prince Leader?'

'Do I ever.' Charmers sighed with relief and used the space that the two incredible pilots had bought her to pull her Spitsteam around towards the Prussian bombers.

Schmidt watched from the shadows at the back of the hangar as the British bombers, he had no idea what kind they were and didn't particularly care, landed from their mission. Everybody was distracted, rushing to reload them as quickly as possible it was time.

He straightened the uniform he had taken from one of the men he had killed, tugging a tunic that wasn't nearly big enough for him into some semblance of decency and adjusting the strap of the British issue rifle over his shoulder, then strode into the light, head held high. In his experience, a confident attitude would hide any shortcomings in his attire and nobody even looked his way as he crossed the empty hangar nearest the huge door through which the aircraft took off and landed. However, he suspected that, no matter how good his disguise or how confident he was, there was no way he was going to be able to just walk across the runway without being challenged.

He was right, and he had barely stepped across the white line marking the edge of the tarmacked landing strip when a shout came from one of the two guards standing by the lift, fifty metres away.

'Oi! You!'

He kept walking, acting casually and deliberately didn't look in their direction, although his every sense was focussed on them. They would be as much puzzled by his behaviour as worried and it would take them a few seconds to decide what to do.

'Oi!'

One of the guards started towards him and that was his signal to start running.

The guard broke into a run as well, but he was slow because he was struggling to bring his rifle off his shoulder at the same time. The man should have run, or stopped and unsling the gun ready to shoot, doing both spoke to inexperience and gave him another few seconds to get closer to his goal.

'Stop, or I'll shoot!'

Schmidt couldn't help laughing, even though it cost him some of his advantage; the amateurish behaviour of the guards in the base was unbelievable! If it hadn't been for those two harpies…

Loud bangs sounded as the man finally did what he should have done almost fifteen seconds before. Most of the shots went wide, as the guard had tried to fire whilst still running, but one went through Schmidt's leg. He gasped and stumbled, but gritted his teeth and forced himself to take the last two steps he needed.

He tumbled to the floor and slid into cover. The explosives were already prepared and he hurriedly planted them on the mechanism, packing them into the openings and around the welding points to do the maximum damage. With his men dead he couldn't hope to escape the base, but he refused to spend the rest of the war in a prison and at least this way he could deny the British their base before he joined them.

He stood up, coming out from behind the mechanism and thrust his fist into the air proudly.

'For the Kaiser!'

The British soldier had finally stopped and taken up a decent firing stance, but Schmidt was enveloped in white heat before he got the chance to shoot.

The five Misfits ran amok among the bombers, destroying them almost as easily as they did the fighters, and things only got worse for the Prussians once Gwen and Abby joined the fight. However, most of the British fighters ran out of ammunition long before they reached Gibraltar, leaving only Abby and Gwen to harass the Prussians.

Gwen used her few remaining cannon rounds on a bomber just as it released its payload and smiled grimly in satisfaction as it started a deceptively lazy spiral towards the sea.

'I'm almost out, Leader.'

'So am I, Two. Let's see this last lot off, then join everyone else.'

'Roger.'

The bombers turned for home, diving to gather speed in an attempt to get away from the Misfits. Gwen poured the last of her machine gun rounds into one of them, but she ran out before she saw any real results and had to give up the chase. She pulled up and disengaged, then accelerated back towards the Rock.

The Nelsons had been rearmed and ready to make another run at the tanks for a good fifteen minutes and their leader had been swearing at Buttress almost that whole time to let them out, but with the Prussian bombers so close the hangar doors had had to remain closed. With the enemy now in full retreat they could finally take off and they came bursting out of the mountain, their engines roaring loudly as if the aircraft themselves were annoyed at the delay. As soon as they were out of the way, the fighters came racing in, the Misfits and the surviving Spitsteams slewing into their places in the hangar spaces so that the swarming fitters could get them ready to go back out as quickly as possible in case they were needed.

Gwen hopped down from Excalibur as soon as she'd handed her over to Giuseppe, but, instead of going to join the rest of the pilots, she strode over to the edge of the runway and peered back towards the hangar door. Something had caught her eye as she'd entered the mountain, but she hadn't been able to get a good look at whatever it was. She did so now, though, slotting lenses in place to get a better look.

'What's wrong, Gwen?' Abby asked, joining her.

'Look. Something's happened to that bloody capstan.'

Abby followed the direction of her gaze, also using the lenses in her helmet to get a closer look. 'That's pretty damn destroyed.' She grinned. 'Some pilot probably got fed up of their little joke and decided to get some revenge. What a shame!'

'Group Captain!'

They looked around as Higgins came jogging towards them.

Abby nodded. 'Marshal. The battles not going too badly, I don't think...'

'Yes, yes, not bad.' Higgins cut her off and thrust a scrap of message paper at her. 'This came half an hour ago.'

Gwen wondered what was so urgent that the base commander had had to interrupt Abby so abruptly, or why he'd felt the need to use her rank, when before he'd always been so informal. Whatever it was, it had to be bad, because all colour drained from her wingmate's face as she began reading.

She reached out and put her hand on her arm. 'Abby? What is it? Is it Jimmy? Has something happened to him?'

Abby shook her head. 'No, it's not... I...' She drew in a ragged breath, then started to go, so distracted she failed to say anything to Higgins. 'Come on, everyone needs to hear this.'

Gwen and Higgins followed her as she clomped heavily towards where the other pilots had gathered around a portable tea urn.

Gwen had never seen Abby so shaken up, not even after the deaths of Mac, Charles or Monty. She wasn't the only one who could see it, though, and the pilots went silent, their smiles vanishing completely as the two pilots approached.

'Oh, no. Not Jimmy.'

Scarlet echoed Gwen's thought, but Abby shook her head and smiled weakly at her. 'It's not Jimmy, it's this.' She showed them the paper that Higgins had given her, then read from it.

'Recruitment request denied...'

She was cut off as protests arose from the pilots, many of whom looked to Eulalia with sympathy.

'I haven't finished!'

Her harsh voice stopped the pilots in their tracks and they stared at her in surprise. She ignored them, though, and looked down at the paper once more. 'Recruitment request denied. Due to Malta failure Badger is disbanded effective immediately.'

She lifted her eyes, expecting comments, but the pilots were far too shocked to say anything and just stared at her incredulously, so she finished the message. 'Return home with Convoy G arrival imminent.' She looked up at them again. 'It's signed "WARM."'

'Bloody Cummerbund got his way.'

Bruce's growled statement opened the floodgates for the rest of the Misfits to start loudly complaining. Eulalia, however, merely walked away, ignoring Kitty's attempts to call her back.

'So, what are we going to do about this?' Wendy asked, her hands on her hips, chin jutting out aggressively. 'I for one don't fancy going back to work for the government, not with that berk in charge of the war effort. And I'm not letting *anyone* take Dreadnought away from me.'

'I'm not sure there is anything we can...' Abby started, but paused when a woman sprinted up to Higgins, brandishing another message slip.

'Oh no.' Owen groaned. 'What now?'

Higgins' eyes widened in surprise. 'It's nothing bad, actually. It's from the King. It says to go and see him as soon as you get back to England.'

Slow smiles began to creep onto the faces of the pilots; the King would sort everything out.

CHAPTER 13

The Misfits weren't going to stop fighting just because of a little thing like the War Minister ordering them to be disbanded and they joined the Spitsteams for their next sortie.

The noise from the battle could be heard from inside the mountain, even with the hangar door closed, as the Prussian tanks duelled with the British army and navy, but it wasn't until they got into the sky that they could see what was going on.

The scene was actually rather reminiscent of France in the early days of the war, when the Prussians had sent their full might against the last pocket of real resistance on the continent. Masses of armoured vehicles were crisscrossing the isthmus, firing their cannons and machine guns, filling the air with smoke, earth and fire. However, whereas in France they had been constantly moving forwards, rolling over British and French positions, here their movements seemed aimless, purposeless.

'They can't get through!' Derek crowed. 'They've been stopped by my trench!'

'Your what, Four?' Abby asked.

'When I got them to update the defence plans, I suggested they build a deep ditch right across the narrowest part of the isthmus, reinforced with steel and concrete. It's too wide for anything smaller than a Goethe to cross, but narrow enough that if a tank does go into it, it'll go nose down and get stuck. You can see a couple of them who've done just that!'

Abby chuckled. 'So we've got all the time in the world to take them apart one by one.'

'I wouldn't say that, Leader; they'll get across it when they bring up something like a bridging machine or a Walker. They're contained for now, though.'

'Then let's make the best of the situation while we can!'

Abby led them around in a wide arc over the sea then brought them in to sweep across the isthmus. As before, the plan was to go for those vehicles that were in the front ranks, not because they were the biggest threat, but because their destruction would create obstacles for the ones following.

There was no hiding from the cannons of the fighters and they spread destruction amongst the tanks, but, once more, they barely made a dent in the Prussian numbers. However, the attack proved the last straw for the enemy, they seemed to lose their taste for the fight and turned to stream away, back towards the north.

The tanks didn't return that day, they just took up positions twenty miles away, out of range of the remaining British guns, but the bombers came back twice more and each time the fighters were sent up to meet them. It was impossible to stop them from reaching their targets, though, much as it had been with the massed raids over London, and ship after ship was destroyed, disabled, or sunk and the guns on the wall were put out of action one by one.

Things were beginning to look dire indeed and it was clear that if the Prussians continued their bombing campaign for very much longer then there would be nothing left to stop them from bridging the trench.

Everything was about to change, though.

Higgins came into the Misfits' ready room while they were resting after repelling the second bombing raid in the mid-afternoon. He grabbed some tea from the steward taking care of the small buffet by the door, then flopped down on one of the armchairs near the Misfits and smiled at them while he dunked a biscuit in his mug.

The pilots eyed him warily, wearily.

'What is it now, Bob?' Scarlet asked. 'Are we abandoning Gibraltar like we did Malta?'

Higgins shook his head. 'Perish the thought! No, we've...' He squeaked and swore as the biscuit in his hand disintegrated, half of it plopping into his tea and splashing him with hot liquid. He grabbed a napkin from the table and started mopping at his lap while the pilots watched him, amused.

He finished and chucked the napkin back on the table before looking up. He grinned sheepishly when he saw that they were watching him. 'Sorry about that. As I was saying, we've received word that the War Ministry have actually done something good for once. They were keeping their cards close to their chest, but now that it's almost here they've informed us that "Convoy G" is actually "*Taskforce G*". It's not one of our regular convoys at all, but rather quite a lot of reinforcements with an eye to eventually taking back Malta. Not only are there a couple of battleships, which will move in close and help us defend the isthmus, but the *Steady* is coming as well. She'll stay in the Atlantic with the rest of her group, out of sight of land, and launch her fighters against the aircraft coming from Tangiers.'

'The Steady? That's the sister ship to the *Heart of Oak*, right?' asked Gwen. She wasn't really up to date on the ships the Royal Navy had, never having been interested in nautical matters. The first time she'd been on a ship had actually been when they Misfits had been taken to Muscovy by the Arturo. Until then, if she'd needed to travel anywhere she'd flown.

'That's right,' said Higgins as he reached for a biscuit to replace the one that was a sodden lump at the bottom of his mug.

The HMS Heart of Oak had been sunk in the Mediterranean a few months earlier, on its way to reinforce Malta. She had carried fifty aircraft and if she'd made it to Malta the outcome of the conflict might have been very different.

'It's not just the navy who are getting reinforced. The army are getting a few big guns, many of which are big enough to come up here and replace the ones the Prussians blew up. More importantly, though, *I'm* getting two more Spit squadrons, two Harry squadrons and four whole Splendid squadrons! The Spits and Harrys have actually already taken off from the Steady and will be here in less than an hour!'

Abby laughed. 'Sounds like you don't need us, then!'

'Well...' Higgins smiled sadly at her over his mug. 'Orders came in for you at the same time. You're done here, I'm afraid. Your aircraft are to be disassembled immediately and you are to be ready for embarkation after dark tonight. You leave at three in the morning.'

The Misfits stood on what remained of the observation platform on the summit of the Rock, surrounded by the ruins of the gun batteries and with the melted remains of Victor and Victoria at their backs.

The mood was sombre as they watched the sun go down, not just because they were leaving, but because they had been forced to stand by and watch the ten surviving Spitsteams go out to face the last

Prussian raid of the day on their own. The fighter squadrons from the Steady had arrived in dribs and drabs before the raid, but they'd been launched at the limit of their range, without any ammunition to save weight, and there had been no time to get them rewound and rearmed before the bombers arrived. Three of the Spits hadn't come back, one of them Charmers'.

Their view was partially obstructed by smoke rising from the fires raging below, but it did very little to hide the devastation the Prussians had caused.

A few errant shots from the Goethes had hit the northernmost part of the town the day before, but the damage they had done was negligible compared to that caused by the bombers. The warships had been bunched up close to the town so they could bring their guns to bear on the tanks and that had made them easy targets. Very few of the vessels had escaped unscathed and more than half a dozen were burning wrecks or on their way to the bottom of the bay. The town itself had suffered considerably as well, especially around the port, and the fire control crews were being overwhelmed due to the nature of the old buildings and the way they were packed so closely in the tiny space.

Gibraltar would survive, though. The reinforcements would be more than enough to at least hold the isthmus, if not drive the Prussians away outright, the air base was still completely functional, there were already replacement guns for the mountain in the convoy, and the houses could always be rebuilt. If anything, the British would have a stronger position than ever.

Which meant that, much as the Misfits hated to have to leave others doing the fighting and dying and the War Minister for making them do so, they were no longer needed.

When the last sliver of the sun had disappeared behind the Spanish mainland across the bay and the sky had begun to darken behind them in the east, the Misfits stirred uneasily, knowing they had to go, but unwilling to do so.

'Well, at least we haven't lost anyone else,' said Owen, wryly.

'That's because we haven't bloody done anything.' Bruce replied. He was particularly grumpy because the lovely Captain Perdita Brown was stuck at the front and wouldn't be able to join them for the goodbye meal they had organised in the mess.

'We did what we could, Bruce,' said Abby, 'but yes, it looks like we're going to have to let someone else be the heroes this time.'

'Yes!' Owen cried out, smiling widely, 'and *they* can be sent on the next suicidal mission instead of us!'

There was a half-hearted cheer at that, but their hearts weren't in it and silence quickly fell once again.

Abby turned to Eulalia.

'Are you sure you won't come with us?

'No. Thank you, but my place is here.' She looked north, towards her home in Catalunya. 'When the fight here is done, I have another to go back to.' She smiled. 'But one day I might just turn up on your doorstep asking for a job.'

'You'd be more than welcome. You'll dine with us tonight, though, won't you?'

'Of course! This is my last chance to eat and get drunk on the Misfits' bill!'

Gwen stood to one side with Kitty, listening to the others talk. She snuggled in to the American's side and peered up at her in the fading light. 'It's a pity Eulalia's not coming with us; she's a really good pilot.'

Kitty smirked down at her. 'I would have thought you'd be happy she's not.'

Gwen thought for a second, then shook her head and grinned. 'If you'd asked me a few days ago I might have been, but after the last few nights I'm almost convinced you no longer have feelings for her.'

Kitty raised an eyebrow. 'Almost?'

'Almost.'

'Well, I don't know how much privacy we're going to get on the ship, but how about I start convincing you right now...' She bent down and softly kissed Gwen.

Gwen wanted to relax and enjoy the moment and she tried hard to do so, but it was impossible and she gently pulled back after a few seconds.

Kitty didn't protest; she knew how worried Gwen was, how worried they all were about the squadron's uncertain future, instead she just moved to stand behind her and wrapped her arms around her as they looked out into the burgeoning night.

Silence fell as the Misfits watched the colours fading, but then Abby sighed. She moved away from the twisted safety rail and began picking her way through the debris back towards the lifts. 'Come on then, you lot, dinner time. We don't want to keep our guests waiting.'

What few personal effects they had were already packed and after a dinner, which was all too brief, they made their way down to the port and their assigned embarkation point. There, they boarded a launch, which carried them out to the troop ship taking them back to Britain, along with the injured who were being evacuated.

No lights were on in any of the ships and strict blackout rules were in place, so the Misfits had no last sight of Gibraltar, beyond the deep black shadow of the looming Rock.

Gruber skimmed through the casualty reports for the previous day, bypassed the readiness reports entirely and barely glanced at the stores reports. He threw the papers down, then took another sip of his coffee before looking up at the two men standing to attention in front of his desk.

They looked nervous, and well they might; they had failed him.

'So, and please feel free to correct me if I'm wrong, you're telling me that it is impossible to take Gibraltar.'

'Yes, sir.' The army general in charge of the armoured divisions said. Gruber had been introduced to him of course, but couldn't remember his name. Panda, Painter, Panzer... something like that - he hadn't really been paying attention; he'd been too busy flirting with the girl serving the drinks. 'Not only did we suffer heavy losses in our failed attack, but the British have been reinforced. They now have several more squadrons of fighters and our observers report an entire task force, including the HMS Steady, has anchored in the bay. The guns of their ships will easily be able to destroy our Walkers and bridging vehicles and we won't be able to get across that trench.'

Gruber sighed. 'Then I suppose I will have to do this myself. After breakfast I will take my Barons back into the fight. We will destroy the Misfits and I will personally defeat Stone and Lennox. That will demoralise the British and you can go back in after our bombers have dealt with their ships.'

The men glanced at each other and he scowled. 'What? What else? What aren't you telling me?'

'The Misfits aren't there anymore,' said the general.

'What?' Gruber banged his coffee cup down on the table, spilling the dregs over the paperwork, and surged to his feet.

The two men recoiled slightly, well aware of what happened to people who displeased Hans Gruber, the Kaiser's favourite. The general pressed ahead, though, valiant in the face of danger. 'Our spy in Gibraltar sent an urgent message yesterday evening saying that the pilots would be boarding a ship for evacuation to Britain. They left last night and will be hundreds of miles into the Atlantic by now.'

'Well, hunt that ship down and sink it, then!' Gruber shouted, staring at the other man, his liaison with the few naval forces in the Mediterranean.

The man shook his head fearfully. 'We can't, sir. They have too big a lead and besides, it would be like looking for a needle in a haystack.'

Gruber slammed his fists down on the table, then stalked over to the window. He looked out at the airfield and the neat row of red aircraft he'd insisted be parked opposite his office so that he could look out at them whenever he wanted.

'Very well. There is no longer any point in my being here. General, you are now in charge, continue the attack as you see fit, or don't. I really don't care.'

'But...'

The general began to protest, but Gruber just grabbed his few personal effects from the desk, dumped them into his bag, then barged out, leaving the two men gaping after him.

EPILOGUE

25th June 1941

It wasn't until the Misfits were sitting comfortably around a small dining table in one of the many lounges of Buckingham Palace, with tea and cucumber sandwiches in front of them, that the King finally got down to business. Unfortunately, any good feeling the ten pilots had at his warm welcome or their reception by the people of England was destroyed by his first words to them.

'I'm sorry, but there's nothing I can do.'

He held up a hand to forestall them before they could say anything.

'Let me clarify - I can't do anything *right now* because at the moment the War Minister is too highly regarded. The last few weeks, the things he's been doing have actually made some sense, like that convoy to Gibraltar, and people are forgetting all the silly stuff he's done. So, until he slips up again, which I don't doubt he will do, or realises how much we actually need you, we just have to bide our time.'

'What are we supposed to do until then, sir?' asked Abby. 'It wouldn't do my pilots *any* good to sit on their thumbs.'

The King smiled at her. 'No, of course not. Nor will I let you be simply torn apart and scattered to the winds in whatever squadrons the War Minister desires. Which is precisely why I have insisted that Sir Douglas promote you all regularly, *Dame* Lennox. And by the time you leave this room, those of you who weren't already will be sufficiently high-ranked that you can't just be sent off willy nilly.'

'Oh goody!' Scarlet clapped her hands delightedly. 'A pay rise!'

The King laughed. 'Indeed, *Squadron Leader* Flynn.'

The Irishwoman grinned wolfishly. 'An extra stripe is wonderful, thank you, sir! But you know what would really set my uniform off? One of those lovely sashes you gave Abby...'

'Don't push your luck!'

'Yes, sir.' Scarlet said, pouting, to more laughter.

The King took a sip of his tea, then set it aside. He glanced over his shoulder and the Marshal of the Court stepped forward and placed a stack of buff-coloured folders on the table in front of him.

The King tapped the folders. 'In here are the details of your various assignments. I hope they will be to your liking.'

He started handing them out. '*Squadron Leader* Wendy Llewellyn, head of her own weapons research department. *Group Captain* Owen Llewellyn, head of *his* own radar research department in the same facility.'

The King beamed when Owen and Wendy looked at each other happily, then turned to Scarlet

'Officially you're to become an instructor at Infiltration and Sabotage, but unofficially you'll be part of a newly formed unit called the "Tactical Air Squadron". I'm sure they'll have lots of interesting things for you to do.'

Scarlet's eyes lit up as she took her folder. 'If they don't, I'll make sure to find something for them!'

The King grinned, his eyes sparkling. 'The Prussians won't know what hit them!' He handed the next folder to Bruce. '*Squadron Leader* Walker, you'll be taking command of a new squadron being formed with your fellow countrymen. I think you'll find a few familiar names among them. Fifth page.'

He waited while Bruce opened the folder and turned the papers until he came to a list of names. The Australian smiled; there were indeed some he recognised. 'Thank you, sir!'

'Next!' The King said, looking at Drake, Tanya and Derek one by one. 'Squadron Leader Drake, your temporary rank has been confirmed. Welcome to Britain and the Royal Aviator Corps, *Aviator Lieutenant* Guseva. Good to see you again, *Squadron Leader* Niven. You three will be taking up positions as instructors at the Officer Orientation College where you'll each have a chance to impart your *unique* skills to the young men and women and hopefully improve their chances of survival.'

As the three pilots took their folders, the King pushed the next one over to Abby, but, before he could say anything, she gently put her hand on it. 'If you're planning on promoting me to a desk, sir, then I respectfully refuse; I belong in the air.'

'Well, I was going to make you the RAC's liaison with the War Minister...'

Abby stared at him, horrified, and he chuckled. '... but I suppose you'll have to make do with what's in there.'

The other pilots chuckled, not unkindly, as Abby finally opened the folder.

'You'll remain a Group Captain, for now at least, because a promotion would definitely put you behind that desk you so fear, but you'll be taking command of Biggin Hill. Reginald Brice is long due a promotion and he'll be moving on and upwards, so we need someone to take over. It'll mean a bit more paperwork and at least a couple of hours a day on your arse, but you'll retain flying privileges and I've wangled it so you get to keep Dragon.'

Abby beamed. 'Thank you, sir!'

'You are more than welcome.'

The King nodded graciously, then turned to Gwen and Kitty. 'Last, but by no means least, I have a very special mission for *Squadron Leader* Stone and *Aviator Lieutenant* Wright.'

'Anything, sir.' Gwen said, pleased, but not a little surprised, at her fresh promotion so soon after her last one.

'I was hoping you'd say that.' The King smiled warmly and passed their folders to them across the table.

Gwen opened hers and glanced at the sheet of paper on top. It was thick, creamy paper, embossed with the King's coat of arms and her eyes widened when she saw what he had in mind for her and Kitty.

'Gosh!'

ABOUT THE AUTHOR

Simon Brading's interest in aviation began when he was very young and at thirteen he joined the RAF section of the Combined Cadet Forces of Dulwich College with the aim of becoming a pilot. However, when he was 18, had reached the rank of Flight Sergeant in the CCF and was trying to get into a University Air Squadron, he was told that his eyesight wasn't good enough to be a pilot, so he had to move onto plan B... something else.

He tried his hand at many things before it occurred to him that he might have a few stories to tell. He never lost his interest in flight, though, and hopes to add a PPL to his very basic and probably extremely expired glider license.

www.simonbrading.co.uk

For news of special offers, upcoming releases, exclusive content, competitions and events, please follow me on social media.

Instagram - @sibrading
Facebook - Simon Brading Author
Tiktok - @SimonBradingAuthor

In addition, souvenirs and merchandise, including T-shirts, badges, stickers and more, are available from the Misfit Squadron store on REDBUBBLE at

https://www.redbubble.com/people/misfitsquadron/shop

ALSO BY SIMON BRADING

The "Displacers" series - a young adult time travel adventure series for all ages.
The Time Traveller's Nephew
The Secret of the Ancients
The Whitechapel Plot
The Price of Greed
The Time for Vengeance

The "Misfit Squadron" Series - a Steampunk series set in an alternate World War 2.
The Battle Over Britain
The Russian Resistance
A Misfit Midwinter
The Lion and the Baron
The Maltese Defence
Tales From the Second Great War
The Siege of Gibraltar
The King's Mission
The Home Front

The Dismal Futures books - stand-alone science fiction tales suitable for adults.
Empath
The Lifeboat at the End of the Universe

The "Twin Ambitions" series - ballet books for children ages 7 and up.
Fight to Dance
Back to Basics

The "Ni Hon - The Two Books" Series - a young adult series set in a dystopian future Japan.
The Black Book

Others
Public Enemy